No Game No Life 4

YUU KAMIYA

ONE HALF
OF THE
GAMER
SIBLINGS HAS
DISAPPEARED!

"My name's Plum… As you can see, I'm a Dhampir."

"Hiii, guyyys!
Tee-hee-hee! ★
I'm Amila,
the stand-
in for the
queeen. Mm,
eeeverything's
fiiine! ★"

Sora muttered to the muscular old man who wore nothing but a loincloth, doing his level best to keep the geezer out of his line of sight.

"Yeees, a feast for the eyes, is it not, Your Majesty?"

"Yeah, if we just didn't have you here, it woulda been perfect."

TAIL

STEPH

"Why am I the only one dressed like you and Mr. Ino—in the *boys' uniform?*"

THE TEN COVENANTS

The absolute law of this world, created by the god Tet upon winning the throne of the One True God. Covenants that have forbidden all war among the intelligent Ixseeds—namely.

1. In this world, all bodily injury, war, and plunder is forbidden.
2. All conflicts shall be settled by victory and defeat in games.
3. Games shall be played for wagers that each agrees are of equal value.
4. Insofar as it does not conflict with "3," any game or wager is permitted.
5. The party challenged shall have the right to determine the game.
6. Wagers sworn by the Covenants are absolutely binding.
7. For conflicts between groups, an agent plenipotentiary shall be established.
8. If cheating is discovered in a game, it shall be counted as a loss.
9. The above shall be absolute and immutable rules, in the name of the God.

10. Let's all have fun together.

CONTENTS
04

No Game No Life

YUU KAMIYA

YEN ON

NEW YORK

NO GAME NO LIFE, Volume 4
YUU KAMIYA

Translation by Daniel Komen

NO GAME NO LIFE ©YUU KAMIYA 2013 First published in 2013 by KADOKAWA CORPORATION, Tokyo. English translation rights reserved by Yen Press, LLC under the license from KADOKAWA CORPORATION, Tokyo, through Tuttle-Mori Agency, Inc., Tokyo.

English translation © 2016 by Yen Press, LLC

Yen On
1290 Avenue of the Americas
New York, NY 10104
www.yenpress.com

Yen On is an imprint of Yen Press, LLC.
The Yen On name and logo are trademarks of Yen Press, LLC.

The publisher is not responsible for websites (or their content) that are not owned by the publisher.

First Yen On Edition: March 2016

Library of Congress Cataloging-in-Publication Data
Names: Kamiya, Yuu, 1984– author, illustrator. | Komen, Daniel, translator.
Title: No game no life / Yuu Kamiya, translation by Daniel Komen.
Other titles: No gemu no raifu.
English
Description: First Yen On edition. | New York, NY : Yen ON, 2015–
Identifiers: LCCN 2015041321 |
    ISBN 9780316383110 (v. 1 : pbk.) |
    ISBN 9780316385176 (v. 2 : pbk.) |
    ISBN 9780316385190 (v. 3 : pbk.) |
    ISBN 9780316385213 (v. 4 : pbk.)
Subjects: | BISAC: FICTION / Fantasy / General. | GSAFD: Fantasy fiction.
Classification: LCC PL832.A58645 N6 2015 | DDC 895.63/6—dc23 LC record available at http://lccn.loc .gov/2015041321

10 9 8 7

LSC-C

Printed in the United States of America

This is a fairy tale from long in the past. More distant than the sea—

Once upon a time there was a beautiful princess. Her hair was so golden as to make the Moon jealous. Her eyes were so bright as to make the stars fade. Her voice was so sweet that it put songbirds to shame. Tales of her beauty resounded across the seven continents. Men came from all over the world to seek the princess's hand in marriage.

The princess decreed:
"To the one who gives me the most wondrous gift—let me grant him my love."
Many men came and presented her with dazzling gifts. Gold, silver, and gemstones were beneath mention. A hundred fiefdoms, a thousand castles, ten thousand servants—all were given to the princess.

But the princess was unmoved.
"Please, I would like something more lustrous. Something still more wondrous."
More men came and presented her gifts without equal. Words of love matchless in the world were beneath mention. Secret

treasures matchless on Earth and divine treasures matchless in Heaven were given to the princess.

But the princess was not satisfied. No beauty was beautiful to the princess. No love was surprising to the princess. No treasure was new to the princess.
—There was nothing in the world that could impress the princess. And still the princess insisted:
"Come—is there not something still more wondrous?"

—And then, one day, a certain prince came before the princess. This prince was different from any the princess had seen before. He was young and strapping, yet shabby in guise. It appeared that he had nothing—no treasure of any sort. But then the prince showed her a small, small treasure.
"Princess, let me present you with a treasure you have surely never seen."
The treasure he held out was more wondrous and beautiful than anything in the world. The princess let out a breath of astonishment. She swore her love to the prince. And the treasure was—

......
"This is it! This is 'true love'!" she cried, slamming shut the book in her hands. And so, seeking true love, she fell into a long sleep, waiting for the day when the man bringing that small treasure she'd heard of in the fairy tale would appear before her.
—Ignorant of what was to come.

What *she* had been reading was a fairy tale. But what she sought through sleep was no mere tale, no story. Long in the past, more distant than the sea, fully eight hundred years ago—

—It was a *historical fact*, one at which no Ixseed could help but stifle a laugh.

⏻ EASY START

Werebeast country—in the Eastern Union, on the outskirts of the capital, Kannagari, there was situated the mansion of Izuna Hatsuse, former ambassador of the Eastern Union in Elkia. Built of wood in a manner resembling the traditional Japanese residential style, in a room fragrant of fresh tatami floor mats woven of simple rice straw, amid stillness and darkness befitting the classical phrase, "The dead of the night, when even the trees and grass slumber," a lone shadow moved.

"…Shiro, are you awake?"

The shadow bounced up from its futon and directed a quiet whisper to its neighbor.

…There was no reply, only the peaceful sounds of sleep. Hurriedly, but holding its breath so as to make no sound, the shadow rummaged by its pillow. Then, having grasped the *contraband* it sought, it withdrew stealthily to a corner of the room.

"Clear on the right, clear on the left—all clear, no one here but Shiro," he whispered, manipulating what was clutched in his hands as his face emerged from the darkness.

A young man with black eyes, black hair, and dark circles under his eyes that ruined his physiognomy. Sora, eighteen. One of the two monarchs of Elkia, the last nation of Immanity. The monarch paid careful attention to his surroundings as, with a tablet computer in his left hand and a box of tissues in his right, he whispered loudly and proudly:

"I believe this is the opportunity—I shall finally be able to release my *venom*!!"

—He was a pervert. Were they to see their king as he was now, the people would surely cry *Alas!* as they wet their cheeks in sorrow. But withhold judgment, if you would. It had been over two months since he and his younger sister had been summoned to Disboard, a world where everything was decided by games. In the blink of an eye, he had ascended to the throne of the cornered human race of Immanity and had played countless killer games alongside his sister, Shiro—games in which they had overcome other races that flagrantly cheated using magic and supernatural powers. Then, they had reclaimed Immanity's territory, going so far as to swallow up the third-largest nation in the world. He, Sora, had been in the thick of those games. He'd interacted any number of times with countless girls—not only humans, but an angel-girl, an elf-girl, and multiple animal-girls. At times during the games, or in the bath, they'd bared their flesh while he manfully tossed sand to obscure his vision and averted his eyes—and though meager vestiges of this Peach Blossom Spring were recorded on his tablet and smartphone, since his little sister was always by his side, until today he had never been able to... er, what's the word? *Partake!* Would you dismiss such a man as a mere pervert?

—Yea, ladies, let it be said: You may despise him utterly. But, gentlemen, surely you can understand?! Thinking of the steel soul of this virgin lad of eighteen as he endured to the present day, can you hold back tears? Is it not rather worthy of respect, to have come this far? Yes, having come this far—is this not what one might call love? His young sister was one thing. But to protect the swarms of girls around him from his own impulses—this virtuous and honorable will—if not love, then what shall it be called?

...Is there room for argument—surely not! Well, probably not...I think.

"Call me a pervert if you will. I can't take it anymore—no, this is a noble gesture!!"

Clutching his heroic resolve to his chest, Sora put his hands to his underpants, and—

"Uh, ummm...ex-excuse meee..."

"Eeeeeeeeeeeeeeeeeeeeeeeeeeeeeeeeeeeeeeeeek!"

Sora fell to the tatami with a girlish shriek at the voice that addressed him from behind. Three individuals responded to the shriek.

"...Brother...if you're gonna do it, be quiet..."

Giving up on *pretending to be asleep* and rising, his sister with her red, half-open eyes under her long, pure white hair—Shiro.

"Mmf... Hey, look, plenty of assholes here already, please. Let me sleep with you bitches, please."

A little Werebeast girl, her black-haired and animal-eared head peeping down from the attic—Izuna Hatsuse.

"Master, is there violence afoot? Shall I slay? *Are there heads to be taken?!*"

The Flügel girl appearing from thin air, a geometric halo floating above her head—Jibril.

Each of their three voices resounded with its own distinct meaning. Rolling on the tatami and fixing his underpants, Sora could not help but yell, "Doesn't this world have the concept of privacy? Is mine being invaded or what?!"

Then, just as he zipped his fly—

"Wait—who the hell are you? How dare you peep on the sacred practices of a wise sage?!"

As Sora pointed and screamed, everyone finally seemed to notice, and their gazes collected upon a silhouette that sat as if melting into the darkness. A shadow in the dark room—so inconspicuous as to be *unnatural*.

"I say," said Jibril as she illuminated the room with magical light from her fingertip and twisted her lips in displeasure. "One able to approach my master without my notice—what could it be but a Dhampir...?"

"A Dh-Dhampir?"

Thereupon, Sora and the rest looked back at the "shadow."

Jibril's illumination rendered just visible a girl in attire so black it seemed woven of night itself. She had blue hair, scintillating violet eyes, white fangs, and wings on her back like a bat's. While she looked like a girl in her mid-teens in human terms, she was indeed the very model of the kind of vampire Sora and Shiro knew from fiction.

—Nosferatu, No Life King, nightwalker... Their countless aliases spoke to the dread they inspired—but in this girl's case—

"I-I can't go ooonn...Pleaaase...S-save...meee."

—Her troubled face and thin-worn voice made short work of that dread.

"Stealthy and phantomlike as ever—unfortunately, while they have the ability to scurry about in the shadows, I happen to have a talent for casting rays of light..." Jibril continued with a sarcastic smile. "I thought you had finally put your talent to good use and *quietly disappeared*. It is my deepest regret to see this is not the case."

"C-casually harsh as ever, Jibril."

Even Sora winced at the insult directed at the girl, who seemed ready to stop breathing at any moment.

But Izuna, dropping silently from above, tilted her head and said, "Yeah, I heard from Grampy that Dhampir had died miserably, please."

"...Huh?"

Jibril's verbal abuse was simply a merciless expression of her true feelings. But Izuna had no malice and was simply using the wrong words. So that meant this was a race that should have been extinct—?

"...Ixseed...Rank Twelve...Dhampir..." Shiro explained, throwing a raft to the drifting Sora. Crawling off her futon, she recited the information she'd memorized. "...A race that survives...by sucking, blood—souls, from other...Ixseeds."

But as Shiro continued—"...the Ten, Covenants..."—Sora grimaced a silent *ah*.

—The Ten Covenants: the absolutely binding laws that Tet, the One True God, had set forth in the world of Disboard. The First: "In this world, all bodily injury, war, and plunder is forbidden." If you took that rule and applied it to the "vampires" Sora knew—in other words, a race that attacked and bit people—that *injured them to suck their blood*—

"Uh, so, what? That means—they can't suck blood without permission?"

The girl's silence, but for the slightest breath, confirmed Sora's supposition.

...To Sora, who seemed convinced by the girl's troubled expression, Jibril nodded.

"If I may add, Master, if one is bitten by a Dhampir—"

"You *become a vampire*, huh? Well, that's par for the course."

Which meant hardly anyone would give permission unless they wanted to be a vampire—

"...Come again? No. Well, that's not the case."

"Huh, what? Isn't that how it goes?"

"Dhampirs suck one's soul via one's blood or other body fluids and develop by mixing it with their own souls, thereby amplifying their power. Meanwhile, the one bitten also experiences a mixing of souls—and falls prey to a *peculiar illness*."

Which meant, as Jibril stated with her sunny smile: "In general, this is absolutely disadvantageous to the one bitten."

"...What kind of pathetic vampires are you?"

May I grant thee immortality and the vast power of the night. A race that didn't even have these seductive words at their disposal was just a pestilence. Having heard the tearful tale of Dhampir, Sora turned back to the girl and swore under his breath. Anyway, that explained why it was surprising they weren't extinct. But conversely, that also raised a question for Sora.

—Why *aren't* they extinct?

"P-pleaaase…I-I feel I'll surely…dieee… Be-bequeath me your soul…"

As Sora considered the issue, the girl started to breathe in rapid, shallow gasps as if begging. True to her claim that she would die, her voice was raspy and cracked—and yet.

"Look, Jibril just told me if I give you my soul I'll get a disease, so why would I do that? Die, dumbass."

And yet—it was quite nasty to wake up to someone dying before your eyes. It wasn't as if he didn't want to help. But, come on, to be a *virgin with a disease*? Sora scratched his head.

"Oh, Master, I did not explain sufficiently. *If one is not bitten*, one is not afflicted."

—Hmm?

"Biting and *sucking blood through their fangs*—'mixing of souls'— is a dhampir's only way to develop. But as far as merely maintaining their life, oral consumption of the subject's bodily fluids will suffice."

"…Your point being?"

"The bodily fluid that is the densest in soul after blood, as well as being ingestible without biting, is—"

Sora's movement after hearing Jibril's next word…

"Seme—"

"Are you all right, miss?! I'll save you right away! How could I let you die?!"

…defied the ability of anyone there—Shiro, of course, but even Izuna the Werebeast and Jibril the Flügel—to catch more than his afterimage.

To call it instantaneous did the action a terrible disservice; this was a change in stance of fearsome speed. Sora picked up the Dhampir girl, carried her to a corner of the room, laid her there carefully, and—nodded deeply.

"I see, they're not vampires. Good lord, she's a succubus!"

No wonder they weren't extinct. Who would let them go? Sora, his mind screaming, started undoing his belt, but—

"...What's 'see-men,' please?"

"...Brother...R-18...is off-limits..."

There were the gazes of two children under the age of eighteen to consider. Or in other words, the signal to force-quit the "tee-hee-hee" event had popped up.

"...Again? Again, really?"

Sora, on the verge of tears, looked to the heavens. It always happened this way. Sora—virgin, eighteen—will you allow your cock to be blocked here? Will you avert your eyes from the countless Peach Blossom Springs, cast sand yet again to obscure your vision—and will you do so for all time to come?

...It's not right. This can't be right!!! Rrrgh! Sora ground his teeth. The mind he'd used to resist and overcome all obstacles! Was it not time to strain it to overcome *this*? Now, of all times!

—And so Sora turned and looked into his sister's cold eyes with hardened resolve.

"...Shiro, imagine someone's fallen into the river with their clothes on and almost drowned."

"...Mm."

"To perform artificial respiration as needed, to remove the wet clothes that rob the victim of heat, and to then provide warmth... Is this R-18?"

"............Uh, no..."

"Right, and why is that? Because it's to help someone! Because it's to save someone's life! Because it's a virtuous act!!"

Sora nodded exaggeratedly, still with the cloudless gaze of a gentleman, at the girl lying in the corner of the room—wasting away in the truest sense, no longer able, evidently, to even produce words.

"Ah, it is true, to human eyes, we must appear insensible. But there can be no doubt that this is a necessary rescue, a virtuous act! And so, Shiro, your brother has no choice! I must cast aside shame,

plunge into the culture of another race, and save this damsel's life!!
So could you look away for a minute, pleaaase?!"
—Perfect Rationalization equipped.
—Let the rebellion begin!

"...If she just needs, body fluid...then what about, saliva...?"
As Shiro's brief mumble brought his Perfect Rationalization (lol)
to the end of its one-second-long life, Sora stiffened.
Jibril thought for a bit, and then, with a smile of one pitying a
troubled race, said, "It should do. The concentration of soul is hardly
on the same level, but it should suffice to save her life, I suppose."
"...Mm, then, I'm gonna..."
Shiro walked toward the Dhampir girl lying at her brother's feet.
And then, bringing her face close to the girl's—
"W-wait, Shiro! That's...wrong, somehow! Your brother won't
allow it!"
"...Artificial respiration... A virtuous, act..."
Sora rushed to stop her, but Shiro looked back at him with cynical
reproach. As Sora activated his brain cells posthaste to rationalize
some kind of rebuff, suddenly—
—*Hey, isn't it pretty much fine for girls to kiss?* It wasn't R-18. It was
totally wholesome. And it was, in word and in truth, a humanitar-
ian act. It is also worth mentioning that Sora himself didn't have a
problem with, you know, a bit of girl-on-girl...
...But *for Shiro to do it is wrong, somehow.*
—Why? Sora shook his head at the question that momentarily
popped up. "No! It is harmful to the moral education of children to
have them French! I refuse!!"
He decided not to think about it too hard and looked around hurriedly. Izuna looked bored. Shiro looked cynical. But Jibril—
"J-Jibril! Give your—"
Izuna was too young; Shiro was a no. At times like this, he wished
Steph was around, but—
"If it is your command, Master—I should be delighted to kiss a
wretched, defective life-form that makes a mosquito look fortunate

by virtue of being able to suck blood freely. But if your wish is to save her life, I cannot recommend it."

Sora winced slightly at her subtly chilling, poisonous tongue, but Jibril went on.

"Were I to give her my bodily fluids, I suspect she would *vaporize*. The receptacle of her soul, you see, is simply not up to the concentration."

—Ixseed Rank Six, Flügel. Why did they always gotta be so, you know...off the charts for everything?

"...'Kay, so...I'll just..."

Shiro lifted her bangs with her fingertips and brought her face toward the girl's—

"———Th-thaaat's righht! We'll use sweaaat!!"

Sora's brain, boiling instantly to reveal the alternative, made him shout it without hesitation.

"S-sweat's a body fluid, too! Howww abouuut it, Jibril?!"

"...That's a good question. The amount of soul in sweat is quite miniscule..."

"Th-th-th-there's no other way! We have no choice but to try it!"

Before Sora had time to move on to some kind of action, Shiro slowly slipped off one of her knee-highs and extended her foot before the Dhampir girl's eyes.

"You will, crawl...and, lick it."

Shiro, Queen of Immanity, wore a smile entirely sadistic enough to live up to her title.

"My sister, your brother always knew you were a closet sadist, but even he's a little shocked to see you have zero hesitation..."

Wincing, Sora sat down lifelessly. Meanwhile the Dhampir girl, who was nearly a corpse by this point, twitched. It seemed as though she sniffed a few times, until, *wham*, she opened her eyes and bounced up. As if flying straight from that position, she took Shiro's foot right into her mouth—

"Wh-what is this? It is delicious, so deliciouus!"

...Everyone vacantly watching this scene had the same thought.
—Ixseed Rank Twelve, Dhampir. Far below Rank Six, Flügel, or Rank Seven, Elf, but still a higher race than Rank Fourteen, Were-beast. The scene of one of these, on the floor, tasting the foot of a girl of the lowest rank and extolling its flavor...

"Is this wholesome...?"
Granted, it wasn't R-18. But somehow it did seem very, very wrong. The Dhampir girl, like a character in one of those food manga presented with the finest dish, as if flowers were about to spring into bloom around her, repeating, *delicious, delicious* over and over as she licked and licked his sister's foot—
"...Hey, are Dhampirs perverts?" Sora asked Jibril, climbing atop a horse as high as Mount Everest.
"Well, that's... But then the souls of my masters must surely be toothsome?"
"—Uh, what?"
"After all, clearly there are few like you, my masters—with souls so resolute, so powerful, so idiosyncratic, so very uncommonly refined, that were one to search to the ends of the earth, there could be few worthy of comparison."
At Jibril's words, even Izuna, who just been watching, nodded.
"...Sora and Shiro's souls...smell clean, please. Not bad, please."
But Sora looked back into their eyes hopelessly.
"...Maybe I'm just imagining this. Is it just me, or are you just saying in a roundabout way that we're stubborn, self-absorbed, twisted, lonely virgins?"
"Good heavens—does it not simply mean that your souls are unknown? Could there be anything more noble than this...? Frankly, it makes me want to take a taste of my own, geh-heh-hehh..."
"......Sora, Sora...Can I take a bite, please?"
Two separate gazes locked on Sora as if primed to drool.

* * *

"Hey, isn't there anyone here with their head on straight?" asked Sora.

"...Are you...one to, talk?"

—Shiro's quiet snark resounded through Izuna's house, which was notably devoid of any sensible people like Steph.

——......

Having regained her strength and a certain amount of luster to her skin, the Dhampir girl spoke:

"Hff... It was quite deliciouus... I thank you for the meaaal."

"...Nghh...all sticky...gotta, wash it...nghh...baths suck..."

In contrast to the girl putting her hands together in ecstasy, Shiro seemed to have regretted her actions—but putting that aside, seeing that he could finally question her, Sora looked at the girl.

"—So, anyway, who the hell are you?"

"Oh, I forgot to mentioon. My name's Plum... As you can see, I'm a Dhampir."

The girl, Plum, sitting properly on her knees with her back straight, continued with a serious expression.

"Todayyy, uh...I came to ask a favooor."

Uh-ing and *um*-ing, she took out some notes or something. Cleared her throat. Slowly putting her fingers before her and bowing, she announced shakily, as if reading from a script:

"P-please pardon my undignified initial appearaaance... Monarchs of Elkia, of Immanity, who defeated a Flügel and the Eastern Union. King Sora and Queen Shiro—please save our race!"

...Sora, appearing to have grasped everything from these words:

"Ahh, so you can drink semen as a replacement for blood, and you need my permission to live—and you want me to *save you*."

Consider, if you will, the type of scenario—the type of game—suggested by these conditions.

How about it? Were you able to imagine it? Sora hesitated not a bit in smiling sweetly—
"Go schlick somewhere else. 'Kay, thanks, have a safe trip home."
"Noooo! Ohhhhhhhh, wait, pleaaaaaaaaaase!"
—and dismissed the R-18 race with abandon.

The grand scheme proposed by Sora to beat this world was a common front that transcended race—an attempt to realize such a thing despite countless differences in background, philosophy, and culture. A construct that flew in the face of the boundaries of race. To realize a multiracial nation. In a world where everything was settled by games, in theory, it should have been possible. This is just theoretical, mind you—but.

"...Can we really count on that lot?"

Thinking of the two who had said they'd transcend race, collect the Race Pieces, and challenge Tet, the One True God, she raised the corners of her mouth. A piece that spoke of a dream that defied all received wisdom. Would it actually be able to fly off the board? Could they fulfill the conditions necessary—? She—a girl with long hair and ears suggesting those of a fox and with two tails likewise golden—considered the matter. This was the agent plenipotentiary of the Eastern Union—of Werebeast—the Shrine Maiden. In the Inner Garden of her shrine, from the railing of the red bridge crossing the pond, she gazed at the moon reflected in the water—and thought. There were many obstacles. To climb the hedges between the races would be extremely difficult even for just two races—Immanity and Werebeast. It was a fantastic feat to bring together even one race under a common objective. The Shrine Maiden had accompanied Werebeast through its internal conflicts repeatedly over the span of thousands of years among countless divided tribes and had somehow brought them *all*—staking everything to the point of forgetting her own real name—into a single nation.

...And because of that, she knew all too well the hardship involved in the task. To then go so far as a multiracial Ixseed nation—that would be impossible by any normal means. If it were possible, by that point, it would mean…

"Well, we'll just have to wait and see a little longer, won't we—eh-heh-heh."

—Looking at herself, one who in the past had spoken of a dream of uniting Werebeast and carried it through, and wondering wryly when she'd become so conservative, the Shrine Maiden poured sake into her cup.

"Let's all, have fun, together…eh."

Uttering the Tenth of the Ten Covenants, she swigged her sake down.

—She'd once sought this, and she'd forsaken it, too. The continuation of that dream had ended—that was *its trajectory*. But this new tale on which she had given up, *they* told full of confidence. And yet—

"Lose yourself in the distant flowers, and you may trip on the stones at your feet."

Anyone could dream. But proclaiming dreams—required qualifications. She could wait until she'd scoped them out properly…to show *the rest of her hand*.

As the Shrine Maiden extended her hand into the air, its palm sparkled with a glow—and the Werebeast Piece appeared. One of the pieces assigned by Tet, the One True God, when he'd set up this world and the Ten Covenants. One of the pieces that sparkled as if woven of light, embodying everything represented by the agent plenipotentiary of each of the sixteen seeds.

—She thought of what it *really meant*, placing her empty cup on the railing, playing with the Race Piece in her fingers. The Shrine Maiden simply looked up to the heavens and laughed morosely at the thing that had made her forsake her dream.

—Hoping to herself that *the time* would not be too long coming.

⏻ CHAPTER 1
ENCOUNTER
THE DEVIL

The Kingdom of Elkia. The last nation of Ixseed Rank Sixteen, Immanity, situated in the west of the continent of Lucia. With the victory half a month ago of the "monarch"—Sora and Shiro—over the Eastern Union in a game, its territory had doubled.

…Its problems had also doubled. Of these, there were two principal ones in particular.

One was the concept proposed by the "monarch"—Sora and Shiro—of a "Commonwealth" in federation with the Eastern Union. This was an unprecedented challenge—to build a country crossing the lines of race. Even having regained some of its old territory, Elkia still didn't have the means to make use of the land, but the Eastern Union, despite having lost its continental domain, remained one of the greatest and most powerful countries in the world.

—Power, currency, and social structures aside, the countries didn't even share a common race or language, and now they were supposed to be brought together on an equal basis. There was no need to explain what a difficult task this was. It was perhaps one of the most intractable challenges in the history of people. And then the second one—

"For goodness' sake—"

The red-haired girl sighed as she stared at the hand of cards fanned before her. Stephanie Dola, also known as Steph. Former royalty—her countenance, overflowing with a refinement that befit the granddaughter of the previous king, still beautiful despite being mired in the deep fatigue brought on by sleep deprivation—yet now twisted in rage, spreading a feeling of disorder. It was because of the second problem. Namely—

"Just how long do those two royal shits intend to play hooky at a time like thiiis?!!"

—Elkia Royal Castle: the Great Conference Chamber. Her roar echoed, causing all present to shrink.

"...Your Grace, I do sympathize, but I must question the extent to which the word *shit* befits a lady."

The one opening his mouth reproachfully, beside and behind Steph, was a white-haired, aging man. His face was puckered with a bitterness that kept him in step with Steph. He had slightly drooping ears, like a dog's, along with a tail. It was Ino Hatsuse, a Werebeast with a physique that was noticeable even through his traditional Japanese robe and trousers. He was the grandfather of the former ambassador of the Eastern Union in Elkia, Izuna Hatsuse, and now, at the unreasonable behest of the absent monarch of Elkia, Sora and Shiro...another victim like Steph.

"'Your Grace'...? Wha—? Did you mean me?"

Ino nodded in reply to Steph's confusion.

"Yes. Considering that this is an official setting, I judged that might be the best form of address. But is there a problem?"

"I don't even understand to whom you are referring. If you would, address me as 'Miss Flunky of the King and Queen of Hooky.'" Steph let out a desperate laugh, but Ino only spread his hands.

"I should like to comply, but then it would follow that I should receive the same appellation... Rather than such matters, Your Grace, would it not be best to focus on what *lies before us?*"

Following Ino's gaze, Steph remembered the situation—and told herself:

"Hff... Yes, I suppose so..."

Yes, right now—they were playing an important game.

The game itself was nothing special, just poker. Other than the fact that they'd introduced wild cards, it was very much by the book. The opponents encircling the table were nobles of Elkia proper.

—Building a "Commonwealth" with the Eastern Union, under Elkia's leadership. Elkia's territory had doubled instantly, and to the issue of just who would manage and utilize which resources and how, the powerful lords came champing at the bit for a chance at these massive rights. At the moment, the idea of an equal, multiracial nation was pie in the sky. You could negotiate over the structures all you wanted, but it wouldn't hold much weight against the difference in the countries' power. Were free trade to be introduced, Elkia's economy would be crushed to the ground. So what should be done with those continental resources for which the Eastern Union thirsted? To say that this one point held the reins over the fate of all of Elkia would be no exaggeration.

—It was a foregone conclusion that the various figures of authority would come swarming to increase their spoils. As Steph had been left with the authority to make law for now, these lords of Elkia appeared one after the other to advance their own demands by challenging her to games. In this way—for half a month already—Steph had been occupied playing games without so much as time to sleep properly. *That itself is no matter...yes*, Steph whispered in her mind. For—*that was the trap.* Everything was as planned. All was on course—yes... If only the challenges hadn't been so *frequent*.

"Verily, Sirs, I am *all in*—will you please just get naked and go home already?"

...What had become of the grace of the lady? With the deep, dark circles of fatigue under her eyes, her face twisted in rage, it was all as if— ...It reminded the lords of their feared *king*, and they looked at one another. Ultimately, they chose to fold—meaning that they accepted Steph's proposal unconditionally. But—clucking loudly, Steph kicked away her chair and stood.

"If you were just going to accept my plan, then could you please not waste my time?!"

She dismissively revealed her hand:

—*Five of a kind.*

If they hadn't folded, just as she'd pronounced—that hand would have destroyed the lords outright, and it made them pale. But with no concern for this, Steph turned as she threw back:

"All or nothing! Why don't you get the *guts to be destroyed* before you bother me?!"

And in Steph's stead, Ino Hatsuse declared with a complacent smile:

"And now, as per the covenant—we shall take your memories. I hope you understand."

■■■

—So, basically, a struggle for power. To administer the land they'd taken back appropriately and make it serve Elkia's—the Commonwealth's—interests. There was no choice but to find someone to take care of it, and if that was successful, there would naturally be spoils to be had.

—That, really, was as it should be. That ought to have been fine. The issue was how the nobles came talking big about whose land it had been originally. In point of fact, the land had been the territory of a number of lords before the previous king—Steph's grandfather— had lost it all. Having had their holdings *unceremoniously laid out as gambling chips*, these men must have had some objections. They must have had some complaints. But—then why, at the time, had they not *stood up to the previous king in a game?*

"*They don't want to take responsibility!* They lose their rights and go wailing about how it's the king's fault! And then when Sora and Shiro take it back, they come begging for the treats. Just when did the nobility cast away its shame?"

"Should this go on, I suspect that the very concept of the nobility might come into question."

Ino smiled wryly behind Steph as she stormed down the hall of Elkia Castle.

It wasn't as if nobles were necessarily bad. Even if they were rotten, they were the governors. They had great knowledge of the management and administration of territories. If they showed the motivation and ability, Steph didn't mind granting them fiefdoms—that was what she'd been counting on. The problem was—

"All these damn nobles who come slobbering—every one of them's got on his face, 'I just want the milk and honey; please don't make me do any work!'"

—And these guys, out of all of them, were the big shots who couldn't be ignored. If you took a wrong step, it could spark a *scramble for power*—a riotous uprising seizing on some excuse to render the state ineffectual. And—

"I wonder if such lords may in fact be amenable to...*being easy to manipulate.*"

The one devising, behind Steph, raising a dusky smile—was Ino Hatsuse. Sora and Shiro were absent, and Steph, the granddaughter of the fool king, held the reins in their stead. Ino had let the rumor out. When the lords came thinking this was their chance to win the spoils, Ino and Steph would make them accept Steph's compromise plan if they lost—and also make them swear to lose all their memories of the game, thereby efficiently hunting them all down. This would enable the policy and concession arrangements planned by Steph to proceed without opposition. It was very efficient and Ino-like—a trap that befit the multi-tribed Eastern Union. But, considering the *mechanism and frequency by which this trap worked so well*—

"They give me no bloody credit at all! What a fine bit of bait I am!" —It was crystal clear how little was thought of her and, by extension, her grandfather.

"Now, now, Your Grace...let's not overlook how successful it's been in keeping everything going smoothly. Let us rather welcome the scorn of fools—all we must do is smile and exploit them."

"...Mr. Ino, would you please stop calling me that? —You may call me *Steph*." Former royalty, head of the house of Dola, Steph did of course rank as a duchess. However, she continued, tired and disgusted, "You make a mere flunky such as myself sound like a person of quality..."

"But is it not the case that, with Their Majesties Sora and Shiro absent, *you, Miss Stephanie*, are in fact the agent of the monarch— the chief minister and current holder of the highest status within Elkia?"

Ino continued theatrically.

"—The Duchess of Dola, chief minister of Elkia, the last remaining nation of Immanity and granddaughter of the previous king. Entrusted with the critical enterprise, unprecedented in history, of building a multiracial nation upon the merger of the Kingdom of Elkia with the Eastern Union. A lady of youth, beauty, and talent...! What do you think? Is this a proper epithet?"

—Goodness, who was that?

Steph looked up at the ceiling blankly.

"So the epic heroine was actually just a flunky. That's a good one. Pretty sharp."

She continued—Why don't you write it down and publish it?—but Ino smiled bashfully and changed the subject.

"Still, to go through this half-month *without a single loss.* You yourself are quite the marvel, Miss Stephanie."

"They're just absurdly weak." Tossing away Ino's sincere praise, Steph furrowed her brow. "To fall for mean, silly ruses that *Sora and Shiro* would ridicule with one or two hundred contemptuous words and then exploit them—indeed, it's a fine jest."

"Well, that I can't deny..."

But—. Ino thought to himself. Steph had, at first, received the support of Ino's Werebeast senses. But as she piled up the victories, Ino had been reduced to the role of an attendant. This girl disparaged herself to no end...yet already she was *more than strong enough.* It was just that Blank was too cruel a comparison. It could now be said that hardly any normal Immanity could beat her. But without the means to know Ino's true thoughts, Steph carried on.

"As if that weren't enough, they don't even notice they're being tricked. Could it be the lords' aim is just to deprive me of sleep until I die from exhaustion?!"

"...Miss Stephanie, you begin to resemble Their Majesties."

—Pt. Steph stopped her feet kicking the ground.

"——Sir, what did you just say?"

Wrenching her head back so forcedly it seemed it would creak:

"That I resemble our *prodigal king and queen,* who dally away the days in the Eastern Union—is that what you said?!"

"M-M-Madam, please calm down! I only meant that you resemble them in your manner of play!"

Steph was winning in a variety of ways—from regular use of straight-out card counting to palming, mucking, and blind shuffling. She saw through opponents' tricks, used them against their owners, bluffed, even played mind games. All of these techniques were tricks she'd learned by challenging Sora and Shiro and losing and losing and losing. It was true that, at first, Steph herself, threatened by the prospect of the Commonwealth's promise fading through her own failure, had thought, *What would Sora and Shiro do?* Yes, she'd imitated their play consciously. But as sleep deprivation and frustration at the pair who showed no signs of returning caused that threat to recede from the forefront of Steph's thoughts, at some point, she'd *started playing as though she were playing against Sora and Shiro.* But her opponents were too weak. She couldn't believe she'd even for a moment compared these goons to Sora and Shiro.

—That *these little goons.*

——Had been *looking down.*

———On her and her *grandfather*—it made her so——

"Ah!"

Suddenly, Steph's face changed as if her evil spirit had been exorcised.

"Ahh, I see. The problem is that having *nobles* just gets in the way of our Commonwealth."

"M-Miss Stephanie?"

At this transformation, Ino queried nervously. But, as if she didn't hear him…as if seeing something that couldn't be seen, Steph, eyes gleaming, whirled about on the spot, almost dancing—

"—Ohh, Mr. Inooo, would it not be fine it we simply stripped aaalll the nobles, the merchants, the guilds—stripped them of everything, threw them into a ditch and ground them to pieces and did everything through the state? We'd fill the gaps in personnel with magistrates selected from among the people, and if they were corrupt, all we'd have to do is flay them to the booone! We'll set up and chase out all the rotten curs who drag us down, and then the treasury will fill, policy will be ours to dictate, and everything will be settled. Right? Am I not a genius?! I-I'm—not an idiot… I'm not an idiot, reaaallyyyyyy!!"

—And she broke down.

"M-Miss Stephanie, get a hold of yourself! What you describe amounts to a purge—a *reign of terror!*"

Laughing or wailing as she bashed her head against the wall and screamed, Steph suddenly...sensed something—and turned her gaze...to see...

—Sora.

"Oh—oh...!"

Where has he been mucking about, dissipating to his heart's content while leaving me to do all the work? Countless feelings arose in her, but before all that, her face flushed at the simple fact that Sora was right there. Her heart's inability to conceal its joy beset her with complicated feelings, but—

"S-Sora! You have returned—ngeeh?!"

Smashing face-first into the column at which she'd leaped, Steph made a funny noise as blood flowed from her nose. She sprawled on her back on the floor, looking at the ceiling...then it dawned on her that the "Sora" she'd seen was merely a reflection in the polished marble column—of herself. She uttered one pensive phrase:

"............I'm just hopeless."

"Miss Stephanie. Why don't you get some sleep? Rather, would you *please* get some sleep? I beg you."

Picking up the limp Steph, Ino continued. "...There's no cause for alarm. King Sora and Queen Shiro, well, they are a difficult-to-understand pair of people, but—" He struggled to find a positive spin on the inscrutable siblings. "—It may be that they are staying in the Eastern Union in order to arrange things with the Holy Shrine Maiden...perhaps?"

A Commonwealth built under Elkia's leadership—of course, it wasn't a matter that could be settled by Elkia alone.

"They must themselves be steadily advancing—a 'summit conference,'" said Ino.

—Yes, that could be. Sora and Shiro's actions always defied common sense. Yet every time, those actions worked in Elkia's favor. This was a fact. It was best to trust them—but—

*   *   *

"...I wonder. Everything they say and do is predicated upon the intermingling of public and private interest..."

It was also a fact that what had always happened was that they found a way to satisfy their personal desires. Casting her eyes in the direction of the faraway Eastern Union, Steph muttered:

"...I'm sure that at this very moment, they're just fawning over girls with animal ears, shutting themselves up indoors, and filling their heads with games like the worthless vegetables they are."

...Ino could find no words to refute hers.

■■■

—And so we take our scene to the Eastern Union: the capital, Kannagari. Equivalent to Elkia's Royal Castle, the residence of the Werebeast's agent plenipotentiary: the Shrine. In its Central Division: the Inner Garden. A space somehow reminiscent of a Japanese garden on Earth, full of fresh nature and red and black. Here, in this place normally off-limits to visitors, a crowd had assembled beside the sacred pond.

"...Hey, Shrine Maiden, what is love?"

"...Tell us, Shrine Maiden..."

The agents of this serious inquiry were a black-haired, dark-eyed young man in an "I ♥ PPL" shirt and the white-haired, red-eyed girl on his lap: the monarch of Elkia and the agent plenipotentiary of Immanity, Sora and Shiro. The crowd consisted of several Werebeasts—animal-girls making coquettish noises as the two stroked them. And there was a line, each person in it apparently waiting enviously for their turn.

"...I don't know, I have so many things I want to say to you..."

The voice that murmured like soft bells was that of the girl who sat across the game table from them. The golden, two-tailed fox whose true name no one knew. The agent plenipotentiary of Werebeast— the Shrine Maiden.

*　*　*

"…Now this has two meanings, mind—what is going on in those heads of yours?"

The three were playing zohjong, a traditional game unique to the Eastern Union.

It shared some traits with mahjong but was fundamentally a completely different game.

"What's going on? Oh, whoop. We win again."

"…This game…is…pretty, fun…"

As they played, Shiro and Sora petted numbers of Werebeast girls and asked nutty questions such as, "What is love?"

Having seen this game for the first time and had its rules explained *about half an hour ago*, they'd already mastered it. In the blink of an eye, they'd uncovered the most efficient strategies, countless conventions, and even devised ways to cheat. But the real question was—. The Shrine Maiden sighed with a weak smile.

"Could you let me in just a little bit on how you managed to cheat right in front of me?"

Even the Shrine Maiden's senses weren't keen enough to catch a glimpse. Sora grinned back.

"How could you say we're cheating? Shiro simply *memorized all the facedown tiles* and tracked their positions the whole time, and I just casually *felt for the tiles Shiro probably wanted*—you can't call that cheating, now can you?"

Right, of the two reasons cheating couldn't be called out, this was one. Because they weren't communicating at all, *just inferring each other's hand.*

"Plus, come on, you're doing it, too. We're even, right?"

And the second was because they were competing with that as a given. In just these few exchanges, for the Shrine Maiden, who had been playing this game for over fifty years—*to be plainly surpassed in genuine skill* and to have the point lead taken from her…there was nothing left to say. This was a defeat so complete it somehow felt refreshing. As the Shrine Maiden thus wanly smiled with her chin in her hand, Sora began. "Okay…

* * *

"So, we've got *three* demands by the Covenants—you're cool, right?" The Shrine Maiden chuckled in resignation, and Sora continued. "First, make an itemized tariff schedule objectively based on both countries' interests."

It was clear that Eastern Union understood the importance of the resources on the continent better than Elkia. Which meant that, to set rates compatible with the mutual interests of the two countries, accounting for their differences in ability, there was no one better suited than the agent plenipotentiary of the Eastern Union—namely, the Shrine Maiden. And as long as those words "both countries' interests" were in there, she wouldn't be able to favor the Eastern Union one-sidedly. *Perfect as usual*, the Shrine Maiden commented to herself. Still.

"...In essence, then, you're *dumping everything on me again*, aren't you...?"

Sora and Shiro really had, in this last month, been working. Day by day, they went to the Shrine Maiden and played games with the fortunes of the two countries at stake.

...Yes, that was some real work. If you overlooked how they'd beaten the Shrine Maiden in every game...and then dumped all of the execution on her.

"They say you should leave things to the experts. You're the Shrine Maiden who built a great country in half a century. We believe in you!"

At Sora's jolly answer, the Shrine Maiden cackled and scratched her head. Restructuring allied states into a federation—Sora and Shiro had apparently used the precedent of the "United States of America" from their world as a reference to propose solutions and compromises for the countless obstacles, while throwing onto the Shrine Maiden the job of minimizing the frictions. Actually, that was the right decision. Sora and Shiro were genius gamers, *not politicians*. But there was a different reason the Shrine Maiden had laughed. It was that up to this day she'd *tried to get ahead of* Sora and Shiro any number of times. This time, she'd figured she could win with a game they'd never seen, and yet she'd got it handed to her. Besides that, she'd tried to set up a number of tricks to bring the Eastern Union out on top...but in the end, she'd never once been able to get ahead of them or beat them. But the policies that had been decided upon in this manner, just as they had said, were assembled through and through for both countries' interests. Elkia and the Eastern Union would both lose in the short term so that they would both gain in the long term. She sighed at the documents that embodied these policies but had no complaints. She was even starting to feel guilty for always having tried to outwit them. The issue was that second demand they'd always add—

"'Kay then, Demand Number Two is the usual—let us pet you!"

"...Pet you...!"

—Yes, it was that every time, they would again pointlessly wager the right to pet the Shrine Maiden.

"Considering you're are actually putting thought into the policy, I can't object, but..."

With a deep sigh, the Shrine Maiden glanced at the ever-growing mountain of documents. *Go ahead*, she indicated, gently waving her two golden tails.

"Wooot! We got this, Shiro!"

"...This, is the day...we're gonna make you, gasp...!"

Watching Sora and Shiro pounce with gleams in their eyes, the Shrine Maiden smirked, and considered.

—Ixseed Rank Fourteen, Werebeast, was a race with physical abilities approaching physical limits. But to achieve this in the shape of a person, it should go without saying, would normally be *physically impossible*. What made it possible was their use of the spirits within their bodies.

...All living beings in this world had spirits in their bodies, even if just a minute amount. The ranks were based on the amount each race had and the aptitude of their spirit corridor–connected nerves—i.e., how well they could manipulate exterior spirits—*magic*. The Werebeasts' aptitude was extremely low: they couldn't use magic at all. However, all living things, even Immanity, had the unconscious ability to control the spirits in their own bodies. Were-beasts attained their astonishing physical prowess by thoroughly exploiting this. The "bloodbreaks" used by Izuna and the Shrine Maiden were prominent examples. Werebeasts were born with the skill to stir up the spirits in their bodies to raise their physical abilities to the level of self-destruction. But the price was the peculiarity that the spirits flowing through their bodies were always in disarray. The effect of this peculiarity was greater the smaller and more slender the Werebeast happened to be. As a result, Werebeasts—especially children and females—bore chronic disorders of the spirits in their bodies...*discomfort*. It was not a problem that could be easily solved by oneself—

......So if you want to know what bearing this had on the situation...

"...Fluffy, fluffy...petty, petty...hee-hee..."

"—!"

Feeling the urge to let out a moan at Shiro's hands, the Shrine Maiden shifted her thoughts to hold it back. Sora and Shiro...the two were *abnormally skilled—at manipulating her spirits*. It certainly wasn't the case that Immanity could see spirits. Even taking into account that they were from another world, manipulating body spirits was the realm of high-level magic. Yet these two—

"—Heh, I think this is the spot!"

"_____!!"

—Instantly picking up on her reaction to where they touched her, they were effectively manipulating her spirits via petting. As a result, they were resolving her Werebeast chronic disorder of body spirits—without particularly intending to do so. What was the word for this—should they be called "celebrity masseuses"?

—Now you see why there's a line for getting petted, right?

"...So, you said today your demands are three... Mm."

Almost moaning at the on-the-spot fluffing but holding back by sheer force of will, the Shrine Maiden asked:

"—Mightn't I get an explanation by now? Of course, it must have something to do with this situation, eh?"

Sora and Shiro were being glommed on to by a bunch of strange Werebeast girls and busily petting them all. That was enough to make her want to say a thing or a thousand, but setting that aside... The two had wrapped strips of cloth, apparently Izuna's, so as to hide their lower faces. In addition, Sora was wearing what looked like fake cat ears, with Shiro wearing rabbit ears. Even Jibril, waiting behind them, for some reason had droopy dog ears on her head, and beside her, Izuna was staring at the girls being petted by Sora and Shiro as if waiting for her own turn. And then the Shrine Maiden cast her narrowed eyes upon the last of their party. Before her shivered a Dhampir girl, crouching and trembling in the corner of the room.

"It seems this Dhampir—Plum—whose 'favor' we refused last night responded by going all over Kannagari telling everyone about our petting skills."

Apparently, that explained the line of animal-girls waiting to be petted. They'd hidden their faces and warped to the front of the Shrine, yet just the short walk from the gate had been enough to produce this situation. Sora spread his hands and laughed.

"She says she's gonna keep interfering with our work until we save Dhampir."

"......I see..."

"Master, do you not feel it is about time? Let us have her wager her head in a game. And then let us ensnare her in the game and take it. Her head, I mean. ♥"

"I-I—I'm sorryyy...B-b—but, you see, the very life of my race is at staaake!"

Shrinking at Jibril's murderous eyes, Plum squealed piteously.

"—So, yeah, my third demand..."

"Mm-hmm."

"Please use the power you've got as agent plenipotentiary of Werebeast and order them to leave us alone until we look for them. Now there's a line in front of Izuna's house. We have a phobia of being looked at, and we can't even open the door. And we can't get on to the real issue, either."

......

—Apparently, Sora had many things to say. Wanting to hear what this so-called real issue was, the Shrine Maiden sharply opened her mouth.

"—Why don't you go."

This was enough to make the animal-girls' hair stand on end with a twitch, and they bowed repeatedly as they fled the garden as if rolling away. Watching them leave, Shiro waved. "Bye-bye."

"Mercy me—well, you speak of something weighty, I hope?" the Shrine Maiden asked with an incredulous look, and Sora nodded back, his face tense.

"Yeah—it's an important issue that concerns Elkia and the Eastern Union."

Starting thusly, Sora no longer wore his goofy look of a moment ago. His face was a mask of seriousness, as if he'd hit upon an intractable problem. *Hmm*—the Shrine Maiden straightened up and faced Sora as he spoke.

"You know how there's this country in the ocean south of the Eastern Union—Oceand?"

"It's our neighbor; of course I know it. Home of Siren, aye."

—Siren. Ixseed Rank Fifteen: the race one rank above Immanity and one below Werebeast. Building a metropolis at the depths of the sea, they could only live in water and thus had few concerns over territory. An insular race with a peculiar mode of life, they only conducted minimal trade with other countries. Just what issue could arise involving folks like that...? To the Shrine Maiden's gaze that asked this, Sora nodded dramatically and spoke:

"Right, it has to do with them, so Shrine Maiden—"

He paused for breath.

"—Shrine Maiden, what is love?"

"Let me give you just one more chance to explain yourself. If it's a fight you want, I'm surely game, though. ♥" With an unreserved smile, but ready to unleash her bloodbreak, the Shrine Maiden growled, her hair reddening.

■■■

—Going back a little to the previous night. Sora, having just dismissed it all without qualification, saying: *Play out your porno game scenario somewhere else.* Holding on to his legs, Plum wailed, looking near tears.

"P-p—please waiiit! Your Majesties, we have no one to turn to but youuu!"

"Shut up! I can't get involved with a race whose very premise is R-18! You ever hear of zoning?"

The race fed by viscous white fluid in place of blood—Dhampir.

—One way or another, getting involved with them was an inexcusable trip straight to the adult corner.

"No! …Well, there are sooome girls who see it like that…"

"I knew it! You *are* straight from a porn game!"

"L-let me explaiiin! At this rate, we'll be wiped ouuut!"

"—Rrm?"

"…Mm?"

Responding to a phrase they couldn't ignore, Sora and Shiro stopped in their tracks. They looked at each other in confirmation.

—Of the fact *they couldn't let that happen.*

"…Let's hear your story, then. Just so you know, I'm gonna cut you off the moment this starts turning into porn."

Reluctantly, Sora plopped down cross-legged, sighed, and opened his mouth. Shiro perched on his lap, and Jibril, following their lead, sat on her heels. Izuna—sleepy after all, it seemed—curled up into a ball beside Sora and nodded slowly.

"Th-thank youuu!" Tearfully, Plum bowed repeatedly. "Uh, uh… give me a momeeent…"

Some kind of irregular pattern rose up in her violet eyes—and that moment.

—Just when had they moved? In an instant, Jibril was right before Plum, and Izuna had taken her rear. The breeze created by their movement blew through the room, seeming a little late.

"…Muh?"

As Plum let out a silly sound, Jibril looked down at her keenly:

"I commend your achievement in approaching my master without my notice, but lest you think I am so foolish as to permit it a second time, allow me to give this advice—might it not be best that you mind your position, worm?"

"Grampy said, if you *sense* Dhampir magic, you'd better get the hell out of their eyes, please." Izuna growled in an ice-cold voice, her suspicions raised.

Sora nervously tried to talk down the tense pair. "H-hey… Don't the Ten Covenants prevent any damage from being done?"

"Damage or not, it is possible to disguise perceptions. For instance—" Jibril directed her profound hostility to a place *beside* Plum. "To make those *voluminous suitcases* invisible—and the like."

With tears in her eyes, Plum waved her hands at Jibril as she stared at the empty space. "It's—it's a misunderstandiing! I just meant to *disguise my own perceptiooon!*"

—From nowhere, a number of bulky suitcases appeared…

"……Mm."

Izuna, her suspicions allayed, sniffled and went back to Sora and Shiro.

"So, basically—she concealed the existence of her luggage to get rid of the weight?"

"No. All it will do is to prevent her from feeling the volume and weight of the luggage, not to get rid of it."

"So when she first appeared, she was exhausted…"

"…because of, this?"

"I-I'm sorryyy... I mean, it—it was heavyyy..."

At Plum's bowing and scraping, still Jibril said:

"Dhampir's aptitude for magical stealth and illusion—the manipulation of perception—may surpass even that of Elf. Those suitcases were *there all along*...and we simply did not observe them."

"Hmm. But you noticed them, right?"

"To my chagrin, they threatened to escape me had I not paid close attention. However, this will not happen again."

Jibril clenched her fists and drooped her head. Sora, shifting his gaze to his side, asked:

"...Izuna, what made you relax?"

"Huh? Bitch doesn't smell like she's lying, please," the curled-up Izuna answered with a yawn, as if she'd become quite tired from her abrupt movement.

—Hmm—Sora and Shiro narrowed their eyes. Before them, Plum was digging through her suitcases, looking for something. Then she cried, "Oh, here it iiis," pulling out a document—

"Ahem, um...I have heard that Your Majesties *intend to conquer all the races.*"

"...Uh, yeah."

That was how it was presented. The fact that they were working on a Commonwealth with the Eastern Union—well, it was probably out of the bag, but anyway, the movement of pieces still ought to have been a secret between Team Sora and Team Shrine Maiden. Feeling no particular need to explain, Sora agreed.

"Let me speak frankly—" As if satisfied by his answer, Plum went on. "Right now, we—Dhampir and Siren—our two races are on the brink of extinction. We have tried everything we could, but...there's no more we can do, so we would like to request your suppooort."

...—Hmm.

"Jibril, you tell me, okay? What sort of relationship do Dhampir and Siren have?"

At Sora's question, Jibril quietly lowered her head and began:

"After the Ten Covenants, Dhampir was no longer able to ingest blood without permission, meaning that their very survival came to depend upon the permission of others—and Siren was in a similar situation."

"...Meaning?"

"...Siren...Rank Fifteen, a race that can only live in the...ocean."

Shiro elaborated. Ixseed Rank Fifteen, Siren—to put it bluntly— was a race of mermaids. They lived on the relatively shallow ocean floor, possessing the upper bodies of people and the tails of fish from the thighs down. They had an extremely peculiar mode of life, as first and foremost exemplified by the fact *they couldn't remain out of the sea for long.* As such, they'd built the ocean-floor metropolis Oceand, claiming a vast marine swath as their territory. Their second peculiarity was existing as *a solely female race.* Which meant their *method of reproduction—*

"...Requires, a man...of another race..."

At Shiro's explanation, Sora squinted toward Jibril.

"Yo, these Dhampirs and Sirens, aren't they kind of ridiculously bad as organisms?"

"Originally—that is, before the Ten Covenants—there was no problem." Jibril continued, "All Sirens had to do was *claim and devour* a man of another race. And Dhampirs could very simply *suck blood willy-nilly.* It is the Ten Covenants that have inconvenienced them—well, races that they have *not* inconvenienced are in the minority, I should say—but the two races that the Covenants have *most* inconvenienced must be these."

To Jibril and her smiling, savage tale of long ago, Sora said:

"...Wha, *claim and devour*? You mean, like, literally?"

For a moment, the scene of a woman, a fish the waist down, displaying a loathsome visage as she messily devoured other races—a scene that looked to be R-18 for a different reason—crossed Sora's mind, and he shivered.

But Jibril shook her head in reply. "No, I kept it vague since you mentioned being wholesome. But I meant it *sexually.*"

"What?? I want in on this paradise! Jibril, let's go, right now!!"

As Sora stood, yelping in delight, still Jibril looked back vacantly.

"You will be sucked dry and die. Is that quite all right?"

"What?? I want out of this infernooo... I'm not going there everrr."

...Mermaids who couldn't reproduce without sucking a man of another race dry? Just how far did this world have to go betraying one's hopes and tropes? Sora, his energy level flung to max then drained to empty in the blink of an eye, sighed and sat down. Disregarding Sora, Jibril continued, "In any case..."

"Dhampir and Siren are two races that *cannot survive without harming another*, and so the Ten Covenants threatened their very existence. Thus, Dhampir turned their attention to Siren."

Hmm, Sora nodded.

"Yeah, guess they would. Since Siren's Rank Fifteen, between Immanity and Werebeast, that means they can't use magic, right? Dhampir's got their stealth and illusion magic skills. They'd eat Siren for breakfast."

As another race on the brink of extinction, their wager couldn't have been too tough, either. It was savage as ever, but when your survival depended on it—. But Jibril continued with a smile.

"Sadly, the story escalates *straight up...* It has become a tale famous throughout the world."

—It didn't even escalate gradually? Jibril continued her narration amusedly.

"I mentioned that being bitten by a Dhampir...brings illness."

"Yeah..."

"Put simply, it is an illness that causes one to die if exposed to direct sunlight. Thus, it is an illness that poses no special threat to Siren, who live at the bottom of the sea and rarely venture onto land."

"—Mm? Hey, so..."

Plum answered with a fleeting smile. "...Yeeesss, we Dhampirs—proposed *symbiosiiis...*"

Jibril took over. "Their strategy was that Siren should grant them blood, while Dhampir returned the favor with magic and would help them catch other races on which to feast. Dhampir and Siren quickly formed a common front."

"That's—how do I put it…?"

"…A—mazing…"

Sora and Shiro together let out an expression of awe from their hearts. Even given that they were stuck in a situation in which they couldn't worry about appearances, these two races had proposed a plan based perfectly in their mutual interests, accurately, and annoyingly—

"Yes, indeed. They are a race most worthy of astoundment—*Siren are, I mean.*"

—What? But Jibril continued, smiling pityingly at Plum.

"For Dhampir, having brought the offer of symbiosis—against all odds, was *crushed!*"

……Huh?

"In the end—Dhampir was *beaten silly* by Siren, and a mysterious contract was concluded whereby the Dhampir males would assist Siren in reproduction, while being forbidden to suck the blood of non-Sirens."

……——Excuse me? This information perhaps not even having been known to Shiro, she gave Jibril a surprised look, seeming to doubt her own ears.

"…Ha-ha…it's really a funny story, isn't iiit." Plum, meanwhile, looked resigned to her fate.

"I imagine our ancestors hadn't thought…the Sirens could *fail to understand* the Ten Covenants and *not even realize that they were on the brink of ruin*…ha-ha."

—Her troubled face was augmented by her weariness as a dim smile emerged.

"…Uumm…? Brother…what…is?"

Shiro tilted her head in atypical confusion at Sora.

"—Ohh…so, could it be…? It couldn't be…" He couldn't believe it, but—. Sora went on. "Dhampir brought them a game where *they didn't use magic*, and they were more or less setting it up for a draw as a step toward a proposal for a symbiotic relationship—but Siren didn't understand what that meant and kicked Dhampir's asses, and there was much rejoicing—like that?"

Jibril's smile and Plum's weary version of the same told him: *Bull's-eye.*

"...Hey, are the Sirens stupid, or—?"

"They are stupid enough to resound through heaven and earth in three thousand worlds. ♥"

"I have to say, they've really reached the very pinnacle of stupidityyy...ha-ha."

"Grampy said they're not even up to the level of hairless monkeys, please."

Jibril, Plum, and even Izuna, who was supposed to have been sleeping, all jumped on Sora's question.

"...Whoa, there's a race that's looked down on even more than Immanity... It's kinda moving, somehow."

Jibril carried on with her tale, still in peak form.

"So, this has several interesting implications!"

Number one—she raised a finger.

"First of all, Dhampir is capable of surviving even on fluids other than blood."

Two—she raised another.

"However, their *growth* depends on blood—without mixing of souls, they will stay children forever."

Three—she raised another still.

"The prohibition on sucking other races' blood only applies to males. However, Dhampirs are not capable of reproducing among themselves while they are still children. To receive blood, the males are forced to obey Siren, and to bear children, almost all the females are effectively forced to obey Siren as well."

And *four*—she produced a finger yet again.

"Even if one were to flee from the city of Siren, one would be a carrier of disease—and you must know what that means?"

And with a smile, *five*—Jibril had her entire hand aloft.

"It means Dhampir unwittingly found themselves trapped by these idiots!"

......At this story, too stupid to even react to, Shiro had already lost interest and moved on to picking at her nails. Sora, too, gazed at the ceiling in a stupor—but then. Through the back of his mind, Plum's words flitted:

—*No—well, there are sooome girls who see it like that*—

...Let's collect and review the information here. First of all, female Dhampirs have no obligation to obey Siren and are capable of leaving. However, if they don't suck blood, they'll *stay children*. Yet *they can survive as long as they have the bodily fluids of another race.* On top of that, the second-best body fluid for them after blood is *that*? And—*there are some girls who see it like that...*?

—Wait. Wait just a moment, if you would.

——......So——legal lol——

"B-but stilll? For a...while, we still manaaged..."

"Whuh, a-ha, uh, yeah?"

Sora had been completely distracted but was brought back in a fluster by Plum's objection.

"I just described the state immediately after the Ten Covenants. Dhampir did, in fact, succeed in *symbiosis, from that point.*"

Jibril, nodding, continued.

"Siren reproduces by despoiling the males of other races of their essence, their soul. However, there were *individuals capable of leaving enough to keep the male alive* while still reproducing, albeit just one such individual in a generation—and so.

"Dhampir would fulfill their binding obligation to assist in reproduction only with that one—she was set up as the queen, the agent plenipotentiary of Siren, from generation to generation, and the only one who might reproduce."

"—Huhhh!"

"...A—mazing..."

Sora clapped his hands in admiration, and Shiro likewise applauded.

"Dhampir just has to assist Siren in reproduction, so it doesn't violate the Covenant. They still can refuse the other Sirens who would suck out their essence till they died, and at the same time, Dhampir can suck blood—GG, perfect, right?"

Well, well—they might have screwed up spectacularly, but that was some turnabout. They'd found a system that would reliably guarantee the continued existence of both races. So in other words, they'd succeeded at achieving harmony across races before Sora and Shiro.

"—Dhampir's got it together after all. Ain't Rank Twelve for nothing, huh."

"Sadly, Master, this system, too, *broke down under the current queen.*"

—Just how many punch lines did this story have?

"Okay, so what did this *current queen* friggin' do?"

At Sora's query, Jibril answered her with eyes half-closed but still bearing a smile, opening the fingers on both her hands. "—*Nothing. At. All.* ♥" At this Plum, as if her face wasn't full enough of troubles, laughed to herself as if ready to cough up her soul as she muttered:

"She said, 'I won't get up until my prince comes to awaken meee'... and went into *crybernation.*"

————Huh? Beaming so brightly one might have asked just what the hell was so amusing, Jibril said, "In other words—"

"The current queen, who holds the power for Siren to reproduce without Dhampir dying—it seems she was influenced by one of her mother's fairy tales while she was still the queen, and so she made this pronouncement by the Covenants and nodded off."

...Hey, wait a minute, you gotta be joking.

"Until the *prince who will win her love* appears—that is, until someone beats the game she's set by the Covenants—she will not wake. And you see, crybernation is a special power of Siren—like the bloodbreak of Werebeast. She is capable of sleeping for over a thousand years—but, as luck would have it—"

With these words, Jibril sat on her knees and made as if to gesture with a fan.

"And now, ladies and gent, we're about to get to the climax of the silliest bit of true history the world has ever knowwwn!"

...Was she trying to be some old-school Japanese comedian? Jibril jovially continued her routine with her idiosyncratic manner of speaking.

"So now!! The queen has set this game—but!

"How in the world is she to *fall in love while yet asleep*?!"

—...There were no words. Plum only looked off into the distance with her tenuous smile. Sora seemed to be holding back a headache, and Shiro by now was stifling a yawn, with Izuna well off into dreamland. The only one still in fine form, Jibril went on.

"The Dhampir men, who until then had only worked with the queen, who could reproduce without killing her partners, and used her as their excuse to refuse reproduction with the ordinary Siren individuals—oh, now! When the queen's asleep, what will happen?!"

And as if opening her fan and tumbling...*whoa-whoa-whoa-whoa*...to the side.

"It's been *eight hundred years* since the current queen entered crybernation. The old queen's already passed, and it will still be hundreds of years before the current queen awakes naturally... As a result—the male Dhampirs, one after the other, *are being devoured*—"

And then Jibril took a deep bow.

"I hope you've enjoyed this true historical farce, stupidest in the world, enough to sweep over the seven continents—because it looks as if it's time for the next act."

"…Welll, I don't know about that, but…yeah, I get it."

No wonder everyone figured Dhampir must have been wiped out long ago.

—But there was one thing.

"If they devour the last male Dhampir, then Siren's gonna be next to perish, right?"

"…If the Sirens were clever enough to understand that…we wouldn't have this probleeem…"

"…What, you mean—they still don't get it…?"

At Plum, who was staring into space with lifeless eyes, Sora involuntarily winced. So, what was it?

"—We are actually down to our last maaale…and he's still a child…"

…So they were five seconds away from perishing for real. That much he understood—but…

"But what do you expect us to do about it? From what you've told me, you're totally screwed."

"Oh, there is more to the story the good Flügel begaaan!"

Plum's face lit up at finally being able to get to the main point.

"The queen is crybernating, but she's *consciouuus*! And soo, we wove a rite to meddle in her consciousness—her dreams—so that it's possible to make her fall in love in her dreams—a romance game!"

…Huhh—they'd brought out a romance simulation game. Sora laughed.

"Jibril, doesn't it violate the Ten Covenants to mess with people's dreams?"

"Not as long as you do so with *no ill intent and no damage, direct or indirect*. In fact, in this case, as the queen is waiting for the prince to make her fall in love, has she not effectively given her permission?"

With a nod, Plum took it upon herself to lay out her request.

"—Please make our queen fall in love! I've brought a plan so that you can achieve thiis!"

Sora and Shiro looked at each other—their answer was already there. For Sora and Shiro, whose goal was to conquer all the Ixseeds—there was no choice but to save them all. But even so, there was one thing that had to be confirmed.

"And *what do we get* if we win this game?"

Plum took out her notes again. "Um…We'll guarantee you 'thirty percent of Oceand's marine resources and friendly relations for perpetuityyy'!" Plum sighed. "…Even just this took us a whole week to explain to the Sirens and get them to understand…hff…"

Huh, those were decent conditions. Not bad. But it still didn't quite…

Sora frowned, but Plum continued. "…A-and also…uhh…"

Embarrassedly twiddling her fingers, Plum glanced away. She looked down at the pile of suitcases she'd brought and with a red face—said it.

"Y-you can do anything you want with meee… Th-that's why I brought all my—"

"Let us tarry not, ladies! There is not a second to lose! We must go to save those on the brink of destruction!!"

—Sora finished his preparations and was set to fly out of the house immediately. And to Plum, with eyes full of compassion, he continued:

"Fear not, young lady. Romance simulation games are my specialty among specialties."

So. Come on, let's hear the details. And then we shall go to claim the legal loli—! Plum's face lit up as she intuited these words that Sora's eyes communicated so powerfully.

"Th-thank youu! Umm, since we're working with dreaaams, we have the freedom to set the scene as we see fiiit, but basically—the goal is to make the queen fall in love and confess her devotion to youuu!"

What flashed though Sora's mind was *Tok*meki Memorial*. The granddaddy of romance simulation games. This confirmed in his estimation—it would be no sweat. Nodding in his head that there was no character he could not conquer, he heard:

"It's a romance game where the conditions for affection are indeterminate and the conversations and actions all happen in real tiiime!"

……Once more, Sora and Shiro exchanged glances. They nodded with smiles—taking the forgone conclusion. *And overturning it.*
"That's a different story. *We refuse.* Have a safe trip home."
"…Bye-bye…don't go extinct…*good luck.*"
All smiles, such was their decision.

■■■

"—Why'd you do that? 'Twas a fine proposal, if I may say so."
The Shrine Maiden, who had been listening to the story silently, briefly offered her thoughts.
"Even I'd always thought the Sirens and all their marine resources would be nice to have. What's there to lose by helping them? And that talk of friendly relations for perpetuity—isn't that just what you lot desire?"
That was the Shrine Maiden for you—she grasped the heart of the matter with a thin smile. This was what Plum had been talking about when she said they had no one to turn to but Sora and Shiro. Dhampir and Siren had nothing to put on the table. The mere offer of friendly relations and modest resources wouldn't be enough reason to save them. If one wanted the territory and resources they had, one could just leave them alone and wait for them to perish. And in any case, there was nothing to gain from lording it over a race that couldn't live without harming others.
—But. As those whose ultimate objective was conquest of the Ixseeds—and beyond—Sora and Shiro alone represented an

exception. Allowing even one race to perish was a problem for them. The resources coveted by the Eastern Union could also serve to fill the gap in power between Elkia and the Eastern Union. And—if things went well—two more races would be added to the Commonwealth of Elkia. It was a fine proposal, one beyond reproach.

—But Sora shook his head with a pained expression and glared at Plum.

"…It's not going to work, Miss Shrine Maiden… Weren't you listening? The friggin' 'game' Plum proposed."

"Mm, a 'romance game,' aye? What's this? You don't like it?" asked the Shrine Maiden warily, still not gleaning Sora's objection.

Tearing his hair, Sora hurled a correction at the Shrine Maiden.

"—No. It's a 'romance game where the conditions for affection are indeterminate and the conversations and actions are real-time.'"

"…Is that different?"

"Hell yes, it's different! That's not even a romance game! It's a 'real-life romance game!'" Waving his hands around dramatically, Sora finally shouted, "I mean, a real-life romance game…is that even a real game?! If so—then what, pray tell, is love?!"

It was a philosophical question.

—But given the assertion that it was a game and therefore having pondered it very seriously, Sora continued.

"If we're talking about a normal romance game, that's simple. Basically, you just raise flags and earn affection points. But look at this. She just said outright, without batting an eye, that the conditions for affection are indeterminate and the conversations and actions are not multiple-choice, but real-time! I'll ask again: Is this a game?!"

The philosophers and orators of ancient Greece must have looked like this as they expounded their arguments. Sora, with a grandness that recalled such times, raised his fists and his voice as he continued his argument.

"What does *romantic love* mean in the real world? Can a game involving the exchange of concepts whose very foundations are unclear truly be called a game? Is poker played without deciding the card values or hands or what to exchange a game?!"

—What, after all, was romantic love? Romantic love—was composed of romance and love.

...Two terms. First of all, they differed in spelling. If they differed in spelling, it followed that they should be pronounced differently as well. And if they were pronounced differently, then of course that should necessitate some difference in their meaning. Romance and love. Then what were they to begin with? Certainly when that ancient holy guy said, "Love thy neighbor," he couldn't have meant, "Sleep with the wife next door."

Yet the Shrine Maiden responded dismissively with cool eyes to Sora's passionate expounding.

"—Can you not just blow your usual load of malarkey at her to make her fall for you? Isn't that precisely what you frauds are good at?"

But to this, shaking their heads with grave looks, Sora and Shiro answered:

"...No, way..."

"Yeah, looks like there's one thing we gotta let you in on, Shrine Maiden."

The two sharpened their gazes further and said:

"—We are Blank, who boasts a *no-loss* record in all kinds of games, but there are games we have never beaten—no, never even seriously tried to play—because we couldn't understand their rules... just two."

They were—

"—The *game of real life* and the *game of real romance*—!"

We who, in our old world, have carved our blank name at the top of over 280 games. We, two in one, whispered of as an urban legend—we are Immanity's greatest gamer.

—Yet, lest you forget. **In the real world, we are but a pair of virginal, friendless, socially incompetent shut-in losers—!!** Sora and Shiro's eyes declared this—their stately stance, their position verging on pride. They turned conviction to truth, to spirit. And that

truth in turn they transformed into an apparition...shaking the air—

"M-my masters, indeed—what force of spirit!"

"I don't get it, but you both kinda kick ass, please."

Jibril and Izuna audibly gulped.

Meanwhile, the Shrine Maiden and Plum offered more objective opinions.

"Is this what happens when you take your known weaknesses and proudly hold them aloft...? Somehow it's impressive."

"...It-it's a kind of confidence that's quite inconvenient for me, thoughhh..."

"Well, that's how it went down, so we had her chill for a bit on the condition we'd discuss it with you."

"...Hff, is that so...?"

"And with that, Shrine Maiden, tell us what love is."

"...Tell, us...Shrine Maiden..."

To the two inquiring with faces earnest with purity, the Shrine Maiden let out a sigh. Sitting back deep in her chair and playing with her tails as if grooming herself, she mused, "—My, my, now what is it, after all...?"

Her voice was soft and without ceremony.

"As far back as I remember, all I thought of was Werebeast—the Eastern Union... Now that I think of it, what is love, indeed? At some point, I forgot to even give it any thought..."

The sight of the Shrine Maiden, whispering with distant eyes as if reminiscing on the distant past.

—Strange. Sora and Shiro somehow felt a kinship they'd never felt before.

"I see..."

"...Well, I guess, that's...that."

So they sighed together and then turned back to Plum.

"Sorry, Plum, you're out of luck for now. Don't go extinct?"

"...Stay, strong?"

Plum, casually forsaken for the third time, screamed with an expression as if about to erupt in tears. "Were you even listening to me? I said I brought a plan so that you can do iiit!"

Her voice trembling on the verge of a breakdown, Plum pointed to her notes.

"It-it's not as if we Dhampirs have just been quietly letting ourselves be devoured all this tiiime... We've analyzed the queen—the 'game'—over a period of many years, and at looong last, we've come up with a *foolproof plaaan!*"

But it seemed both Sora and Shiro had by now completely lost interest. Taking the Shrine Maiden's lead, they searched for split ends in their hair as they responded absently, "...If you've, solved the, game...you, go for it..."

Whining, *Nghhhh*, Plum shrieked, "I-I'll show it to you! King Sora!" And she thrust a finger at him and screamed, "Name a person you think would never fall in love with you!"

"Anyone."

"...Huh?"

Plum froze at Sora's immediate, straight-faced answer, given while prodding at his nails. Sora, with distant eyes—with the serene face of a monk who had seen the light—continued:

"The heavens will fall and the Earth be overturned before the day anyone falls in love with me without being forced to do so by the Covenants."

He continued as if elucidating a state of enlightenment—the truth of this ephemeral world.

"—U-ummm...Th-that's really saaad!"

Her momentum blunted by Sora's bodhisattva-like smile, Plum just barely managed to get her words out. Then, to somehow supply an alternate proposal—"I-in that case, is it all right if I use it on you...?"

"Hmm?"

"A spell—to force the queen to fall in love with you!"

—*Hrmm*, Sora spontaneously said out loud. Indeed, if making her fall in love was the condition to wake her, then if they had a spell like that, it really would be a certain victory. If that were the case, it would change the picture in many ways. But casting eyes of doubt upon the claim was Jibril.

"—*Forcible manipulation of emotions*, you say? The Ten Covenants ought to nullify—"

But Plum replied as if she'd been waiting for those words. "Yes, normally that would be the caaase! However, the queen asked to fall in love before she slept—which means we have permissiooon. That's the thing! We can take advantage of that!"

It was the same logic by which they could meddle in her dreams, Plum explained, putting her hand on her hip. The Dhampir's face oozed with misfortune but was now touched with a bit of confidence as she stuck out her chest.

Seeing her thus, Sora figured it seemed she actually did have confidence in this plan. Glancing over at Jibril, he nodded. "Okay, then. If it's gonna work on me when I don't really understand the feeling of romantic love, then I guess it's gotta be a sure thing."

With these words, Sora stepped forward.

"All right, use it on me. Shiro will determine whether it—"

—But then.

"...No..."

Grabbing the hem of Sora's shirt as he stepped forward, Shiro stopped him short.

"Mm? 'Sup, Shiro?"

"...No."

"Mm, uh, why not?"

"......"

Shiro's eyes for a moment—really just for a moment—wandered. The reason was undetectable to Sora, and so she thrust her brain now into full gear to come up with an explanation...an excuse, *something*. And finally coming up with something, Shiro mumbled, "...We don't, know...what you'll do...if you, fall in love...with, someone."

"Sh-Shiro—do you yet doubt your brother's iron will?!"

Sora tragically pleaded that by now his self-restraint should be worthy of praise. But—the Shrine Maiden, with Werebeast's unlikely abilities to read the subtleties of the heart, apparently understood the workings of feelings at least a bit better than Sora and laughed pleasantly.

"—Ah, if it be so, you may test it on me, aye."

"Shrine Maiden?"

The Shrine Maiden continued as if watching something heart-warming.

"'Tis true of me as well that I lack understanding of those feelings of romance. What complaint have you?"

But Shiro, apparently still wary, asked Plum, "...Can, you...un—do it?"

"Uh? Oh, y-yes! Of course I caaan!"

"Ah-ha-ha, set your heart at ease. He's no type of mine," reassured the Shrine Maiden.

Shiro and the Shrine Maiden had somehow seemingly achieved a common understanding, yet Sora remained unable to follow.

"...Hey, what's this about?"

"I'm afraid, Master, that it escapes me as well."

"...? Sorry, wasn't listening, please."

There was no way Jibril understood, giving her likewise quizzical look—or Izuna, who had already been snoring. Ignoring these three, the Shrine Maiden stood up—and took a step. Silently, she came to stand before Plum.

"Come, then, will you try it on me?"

"Y-yes. All right, King Sora, and everyone else..."

Plum, faltering for a moment at the Shrine Maiden's behavior, recomposed herself and spread her wings.

"It's not a spell I can use any number of times without blood supply, so make sure you watch, okay?!"

At the same time a complex pattern emerged in Plum's eyes, a breeze blew through the room. On Plum's wings, black as if woven of night, there ran—utterly different from the geometric nature of Jibril's halo—countless scarlet lines, wavering, irregular, imbued with crimson. These irregular lines, red as if woven of blood, came to permeate Plum's right arm as well. Her hand—coolly yet complexly—began to move. At the presence of the spirits being woven—the rite, forming the spell—the ears of Izuna and the Shrine Maiden reacted finely. But Immanity being unable to detect magic whatsoever, Sora and Shiro were not even cognizant of this. The only one who could be expected to perceive magic accurately and even see the meaning of the rite being compiled was Jibril.

"—Dear me...could it be, genuinely?"

This she mumbled as if genuinely surprised. After an interval of a few seconds, Plum slowly gestured with her hand toward the Shrine Maiden.

—In a flash, with the sound of something splitting, a maelstrom of red light whirled around the Shrine Maiden.

———

......Mm?

"...What's this? Is the spell cast now?" asked the Shrine Maiden, apparently not having felt any obvious change.

Plum, a bit of fatigue seeping through her smile, replied. "Yes! And nowww—King Sora, please approach the Holy Shrine Maiden—!

"And squeeze her booob!"

"...Whaa?"

Sora and the Shrine Maiden raised their voices at the same time.

"Upon this 'command'—the rite...will be compleeete!"

Plum showed no awareness of the reactions around her and only brimmed with confidence at her announcement. Sora exchanged a brief glance with Shiro, and once he'd confirmed her nod of approval—

"Uhh, okay. Shrine Maiden, you cool with this?"

"...Well, I suppose I was the one who said I'd do it...though I can't say it sits well that she didn't explain aforehand." The Shrine Maiden sighed and fanned her chest.

"...This is really tough somehow... 'Kay, here I gooo..."

With these words, sheepishly extending his hand to the Shrine Maiden's breast, Sora, his face a mask of resolve—squeezed tension into his hand.

He almost let slip a cry at the elasticity that let him sink in yet pushed back. Sora was deeply moved at this sensation—still different from that of Steph. But his wonder at the sensation was ignored.

"Hmng...?"

The Shrine Maiden, furrowing her brow in apparent displeasure, felt something go off inside her, and her expression...changed. And then, turning her gaze languidly toward Sora—in a daze—mumbled:

"Wha-what is this? This skin-crawling feeling...it transcends mere disgust at your loathsome smile, incorporating irritation as well—I-I see... Is this—is this what they call love?!"

"Hell noooooo! And hey, that hurts, damn it!"

—The Shrine Maiden whispered her feelings with a look in her eye *as if viewing something horrible*, at which Sora promptly shouted his dismay. But as if she had no ears for his cries, the Shrine Maiden continued.

"Eh, *this is love*. What is it? I'd never have imagined it, yet now I can say with certainty that I am in love with King Sora. Indeed... so this stomach-churning feeling that makes me want to vomit is love... The world is a surely a vast place."

"—Hey, Plum. You failed, right?"

Any way you looked at it, it appeared the Dhampir had blown it. Sora's expression strained the corners of his mouth, but Plum just stuck out her chest with pride and answered.

"Hee-hee-hee, oh, just listeeen... *This* is where the key lieees."

—And now her troubled face sparkled, having pulled off a feat that only a Dhampir could.

"The love spell is one whispered of since ages of old in distant realms, yet never actually achieeeved—"

"...Is that so, Jibril?"

Love potions, love spells—such things were to be expected in fantasy, but...

"—Indeed. Though I am loath to admit it, the principle escapes us all entirely," Jibril conceded, unable to conceal her wonder. Grudgingly admitting Plum's triumph, she nodded.

"As far as I know, a spell to intervene in such a vague, uncertain element as romantic love, which even those in the arts are unable to define, has never been accomplished even by Elf..."

However outstanding their aptitude may have been for illusion, Dhampir's rank was Twelve. While *magical aptitude* was practically synonymous with Rank Seven, the very image of weavers of complex magic, having accomplished what even Elf couldn't, Plum merely nodded as if to say, *What else would you expect?*

"Yeeesss, the tricky part was how the definition of *romantic love* is indeterminate—*it's different from person to person*, you seee."

Beating her little wings merrily, Plum explained. Raising her chest so high one thought one would hear the sound of the air filling her lungs, she continued:

"No rite can have any meaning over an indeterminate element defying definition. This is why all the stuff that was vulgarly called 'love magic' was nothing more than *lust magic*—however!"

"Hey, wait there, Miss Plum. I'm actually more interested in lust—"

Disregarding Sora's interest, Plum raised her chest as if bending over backward.

"We Dhampirs have finally brought it to fruition!"

"......"

And then the magic that even Elf had been unable to reach, that had astonished even a Flügel, was explained once and for all:

"If it's indeterminate, all we have to do is *determine iiit*! If romantic love is a feeling that differs for every person, then all we have to do is *arbitrarily impose our own definitiooon!*"

* * *

——What was it with this absurd logic? Love magic, so common in games, had never felt as wrong as it did today. With a glance over to the Shrine Maiden—who looked back at him as if regarding a pile of garbage—

"…Uh, but this obviously isn't love."

Sora mumbled with rolling eyes.

"No! If the Shrine Maiden perceives herself as being in love, that is looove! For love—*is an illusion to begin with!*"

Whaaaaam. The race excelling most in stealth and illusion—in the manipulation of mind and perception—laid it out without any qualification.

"…Shiro. I have never been as disillusioned with love as I am today."

"…What…is, love…indeed…"

Ignoring the siblings as they contemplated their philosophy, Plum allowed herself to be carried by her momentum.

"Come, King Sora. The Shrine Maiden must now recognize all things creepy as love! The time has come for you to let out a decisive, overwhelming, just all-out creepy line to make sure! Do it!"

At hearing *creepy* chanted over and over, a desire to say something welled up inside Sora—but he swallowed it for now.

"Uhh…'Shrine Maiden, I wanna get all hot and bothered and lick you all over…'"

At these first words that popped into Sora's head, the Holy Shrine Maiden reacted—with a step back. "Ohh… No, Sora, you mustn't say such things—it makes me more and more in love with you! ♥"

"Yo, Plum! You think these lines and that expression match?! You notice she's looking at me with utter contempt?! Dude, she's clearly telling me with her eyes to fuck off and die, you know?!"

Tears in his eyes, Sora grabbed Plum by the collar and shouted, but the Dhampir puffed herself up with pride all the more as she shook her head.

"That is the form of the Holy Shrine Maiden's love. *That's how it is now*, you seee? Isn't it magnificent?"

"Sure, it's magnificent. Now hurry up and stop it! My sanity is getting shaved away at Mach speed!"

—Nay, I say. This can be no love spell, no cheat code...

—......

"Myyy, that was an experience... 'Tis worth living long indeed."

The rite dispelled, the Shrine Maiden's laughter jingled gleefully. Relegating that sight to the corner of his eye—so the Werebeast would not catch on to his wounds—Sora addressed Plum.

"Okay, I get your sure thing or whatever. But why don't you do it yourselves?"

If they had the means to make someone fall in love so unconditionally, the Dhampir might as well have done it themselves. But Plum dropped her shoulders as she answered.

"You see, the last male Dhampir is still youuung... What the queen desires is a 'prince'—"

Spinning her hands around and making some magic circles or something float in the air, Plum continued:

"It's a spell *to disguise perception*... It may be quite the spell, but even so, it can't, say, make the Shrine Maiden fall in love with some rock over theere... It has to be at least a man with the ability to reproduuuce."

—Then, wordlessly tugging the hem of Sora's clothes, Shiro showed him her phone. Glancing at the words typed there, Sora replied:

"Hmm... 'Then it doesn't have to be Brother,' huh. Most true."

—At Sora's words, the Shrine Maiden's and Izuna's ears twitched.

"Hey, Plum, can multiple people go into the queen's game?"

"Huh? Uh, yes. I think so...though it'll take some doing since the rite to meddle in the queen's dreams is already such a big deaaal... May I ask why you can't do it by yourself, Sirrr?"

"Sorry, but cheats are a last resort. If we're gonna do this, I want to check our ability to do it fair and square."

"The trickster has a mouth..."

"Hey there, Shrine Maiden, don't you go talking shit—a cheat is an unbeatable con that breaks the rules; a trick is a method encompassed by the rules that means you lose if you get caught. They're fundamentally different, right?"

—Though the Shrine Maiden and the rest didn't know it, Sora and Shiro—even in their old world, though they may have used mind games and tricks—had a policy of never using cheats.

"A game should be played out for all it's worth within the scope of the set rules. If you ignore the fundamental rules, you can't call it a game. We'll use bugs, we'll use broken characters, we'll use whatever helps us win as long as it's official—but we don't break the specs. That's out of the question."

He punctuated this with a single nod.

Then Sora realized something—and with a look toward the Shrine Maiden and another *nod*, he asked:

"—Hey, Shrine Maiden—can you swim?"

The Shrine Maiden responded with a *shake of her head*. "—Even if I cannot, 'tis more than enough for me to simply walk in the water. What of it?"

"I was thinking if it's okay with you, we'll take her up on her offer—and go to Oceand."

"...Hmm, well, I suppose. The reward's quite a nice one, and it looks like you have a chance of winning."

"Y-you willl?!"

"—Shrine Maiden, is there anyone you know who'd be *cut out* for this?"

At this question, the Shrine Maiden paused briefly to consider. Then—her hand placed strategically over her mouth to obscure the smile rising unbidden to her lips as she imagined the imminent change in Sora's expression—the Shrine Maiden announced:

"—Ino Hatsuse. I understand that man has taken *thirty* wives."

■■■

Elkia Royal Castle: the royal bedchamber. Steph, having surrendered herself to the bliss of sleep for the first time in a long time, now drifted through the land of dreams—

"We heard the story, you old fart! Now your fate is sealed!!"

She tumbled out of bed at the explosive noise that rocked the castle and the roar of rage that eclipsed even that.

"Wh-what's going ooon?!"

Steph, screaming and writhing from having struck her head, nevertheless grasped whose voice—correction: howl—she'd heard and immediately headed in that direction. That is, she made for the Great Conference Chamber, even forgetting that she was still in her bedclothes as she grabbed her sheets and flew out of the room.

Practically kicking down the door to the Great Conference Chamber, Steph saw what was most likely—no, unquestionably—the source of the boom: Jibril. And perhaps because of it—

"Wh-what is going on here...?"

Ino Hatsuse's cards—he had been playing on Steph's behalf—along with those of his opponents (nobles, presumably) and reams of papers all floated through the air in the wreckage of the Great Conference Chamber. The smoke had yet to settle. And the origin of this calamity, now noticing Steph, finally spoke:

"Oh, little Dora, good day. My masters instructed me to shift us to Elkia *at once*, and as we have a fair number of people, I opened a rather large hole in space. Is everything all right?"

—So had there been a chance of everything *not* being all right? Steph ignored that concern and peered through the smoke. Whereupon she saw Sora, bounding as if to smash the floor—bellowing as he stomped toward Ino with enough force that it seemed he might smash right *through* the floor.

* * *

"Defendant Ino Hatsuse! Charged with the grave crime of having so much of a damn life you took a double-digits' worth of wives! In the court of summary jurisdiction in my head, all members of me, upon my arbitrary and biased judgment, unanimously pronounce you guilty and sentence you to the penalty of death! According to the laws of the galaxy, you—here and now—should become space duuust!!"

"...Ahh...King Sora, Sir, the things I would like to say to you number like unto the stars in the heavens."

Faced with the return of the King of Hooky—and let us also add, the Mad King—after half a month, Ino twitched as he held something back—and yet. A single line from Izuna, who popped up behind Sora, made Ino freeze.

"...Grampy...are you a 'secks monster,' please?"

"Huh—?! Izuna, where did you learn that—?!"

Perhaps not knowing its meaning, Izuna tilted her head.

"...That's what that asshole Sora called you, please."

"Hey, you hairless monkey jackass!! After dumping this mountain of work on me, what did you teach my granddaughter, you bastard?!"

Unable to maintain his exterior, Ino smashed a table apart, bellowing. But seeing this, Sora looked to the heavens dramatically and waved his hands about, pointing.

"Ho! Behold, Izuna! This is the face of a criminal whose grave sin has been thrust before him. Is it not a horrible sight?!"

Izuna, looking disillusioned, mumbled further:

"...Grampy, you're a damn playboy."

"Wha———n-no, Izuna! Your gramps gave each of them the love—"

"Aah, aah! Silence, silence, you slave of your groin! Cease your excuses and take with honor—gkhh!!"

"...Brother...shut up..."

Riding on Sora's back, Shiro's whisper was as soft as the force she applied with her arms round the vexed Sora's throat to shut him up.

—By the time the smoke was finally beginning to clear:

"Eh-heh-heh, you folks are always so lively, every time..."

With a sound of small bells and the noise of clogs knocking against the floor—the golden fox revealed herself.

"Wha—H-Holy Shrine Maiden?!"

To Ino, who prostrated himself the moment he caught sight of her, the Shrine Maiden commanded:

"Ino Hatsuse—we henceforth wend to Oceand, in full force."

She continued in her amused and pleasant tone:

"We'll explain on the way, but it happens this is the time I would like you to display the full force of your predilection for philandering. Have you no objections?"

"H-Holy Shrine Maiden... O Holy Shrine Maiden, to think that even you see me in such a—"

Despite the fact that Ino seemed moments away from wetting the floor with tears, the Shrine Maiden lowered her voice slightly and put the question to him again—

"—Have you no objections?"

—Ino raised his face and looked around. Looking at the faces assembled there, who knows what conclusions he drew in the end—but his reply was succinct:

"...As you wish. It shall be done."

"—..."

Confused, Steph lurked by the door, unable to follow the situation.

"Yo, Steph. You look great. It's been two weeks, has it?" asked Sora nonchalantly, as if only just noticing her. Seeing him, countless emotions whirled in Steph's heart. Rage, rebuke, volubility, curiosity—. But before any of that, Sora's face, one she hadn't seen in so long, made her vision blur. The many lines she'd prepared for when she finally saw him again all flew away. Steph decided to let alone the drops that formed as she clenched her eyelids. She decided not to think about what emotion inspired them, and simply following her feelings, she opened her—

"Aye, policy's been progressing right quick in Elkia, too, I see—under Ino Hatsuse's direction, was it?"

"Dude, it was Steph. We just put Ino there to keep her under control and advise her."

"…Muh?"

—So it was that following this exchange between the Shrine Maiden and Sora, only a foolish noise dropped out of Steph's gaping mouth. Her eyes widened at this explanation, a not-so-subtle change ignored by the Shrine Maiden, who smiled as if grasping the situation.

"—I see, I see. That's why you put up the banner of building a bloody Commonwealth and then, as the would-be presiding monarch, the two of you dallied freely in the Eastern Union… You're as wretched a man as ever, I see."

At the Shrine Maiden's smug words, Sora replied with a similar smile. "They say leave things to the experts—we can always count on Steph when it comes to politics."

"…And when you consider *you weren't present*, all the more, eh?"

"Yeah. What we were more worried about was that some other country might take the chance to mess with us."

—Ino and Steph gasped. But also looking at the papers, Shiro calmly carried on her brother's thought.

"…'Brother and, I, aren't home'…No matter, how you look at it… it's a trap…" She continued:

"…To jump, into…that trap…you gotta be, stupid."

"Those morons don't have a chance in a million against Steph, who plays us all the time—*and learns every time she loses*. Which is why we could relax and focus on the Eastern Union!"

Steph and Ino could only gape, flabbergasted. But Sora hardened his expression a bit and added, "But playing that often is overdoing it. Steph, why'd you *take all the matches?*"

—At this reproach, Steph's thoughts froze. Come to think of it... he was right—why had she accepted all the matches? It was she, the one challenged, who held the right to decide the game or whether to play at all. Why had she exerted herself so? Steph's eyes widened once more as she asked herself this, yet Sora continued:

"Steph—I'm counting on you, but don't push it. Also—like, what..." He scratched his head as if slightly embarrassed, then muttered, "...Thanks, Steph."

—Those were the words she'd wanted to hear. That's all she'd wanted as she'd been pushing herself so hard. Her welling tears, the understanding permeating her brain, feeling her body heat rising, her cheeks flushing—all of this accosting her at once, she still managed to reply:

"N-no... It is only because you two are so unfathomable that I assumed I had to hurry—that is all!"

Sora approached the stammering Steph. Her heartbeat accelerated.

"So, Steph. Hate to spring it on you when you're tired, but like the Shrine Maiden said, we're heading to the city of Siren."

"Eh, uh, all right... S-so?"

Steph averted her gaze. Sora's eyes flitted over to where an unfamiliar, dark girl with a face assailed by troubles stood.

"See, apparently Siren and Dhampir are about to go extinct or something, so we're gonna go save 'em real quick—or really..."

And then, casually as you please—

"...we're gonna go grab the resources and territory we need so badly to build our Commonwealth with the Eastern Union."

At Sora's declaration, the corners of Steph's eyes got a little hotter.

It was true after all. This man had done everything for the sake of Elkia. And now it was Shiro who approached.

"...So, Steph... Can, you, sew...?"

"—Pardon?"

"So, basically, we're going to the beach. Can you make us all some swimsuits? I'll give you the designs."

—It meant, in other words, that her workload would increase again. Steph, smiling, decided to just quietly pass out...

⏻ CHAPTER 2
STRATEGIST
THE SUN

—The beach. One of the top two destinations for rest and recreation, competing only with the mountains. A place where, come summer, throngs of people will gather instinctively, like insects to light.

—In reality, it's a setting where the sand stuck to your feet stubbornly refuses to leave your body, your sunburned skin torments your flesh for days to come, and the salt breeze corrodes your hair every second. When you think about it, it's a landscape whose appeal was absolutely mystifying; a place meant strictly for people with lives. However—even a place as loathed as this can take on a new meaning in a different set of circumstances.

"Hhh... Wiiin... ♥"

Under a Japanesque parasol, Sora reclined on a bed woven of grass with a glass in his hand. At his sides were several animal-girls, apparently servants of the Shrine Maiden, who fanned him with giant leaves. Their short, little Japanese-style coats—apparently Eastern Union swimsuits—opened wide at the front, offering glimpses of their breasts and lower bodies as they slipped smoothly out from under what little coverage the cloth offered, in contrast to their furry ears and tails, more dazzling than the sun. Waving the glass in his hand, Sora thought to himself—this was heaven.

"...King Sora, you seem quite content under this sun... Rather high and mighty, aren't you?"

"Yup! Thanks to Jibril's mysterious sunscreen, formulated with optical spirits or something! But never mind that—"

Sora answered Ino's cool voice in a suspicious tone, without looking over.

"Old man, I'm keeping you out of my vision, okay, but don't tell me you're wearing nothing but a loincloth again?"

"Sir, what an odd thing to say... What shall a man wear to the sea but a loincloth?"

The brawny elder, wearing only—just as Sora predicted—a loincloth, gave him a quizzical "Hmm?" look. With a displeased sigh, Sora pointed to himself and mumbled:

"Look, Gramps. Look at me. What do you see?"

"—Sir, you are of that persuasion?"

"You trolling, old fart?! *Shorts and a shirt!* This is perfectly good swimwear!"

Sensing a voice tinged with disgust as the old man retreated a few steps, Sora sat up shouting. But Ino just shook his head, *Dear, dear.*

"I see a man ashamed to show his meager body. This is quite prudent, Sir. It is good courtesy to hide that which should not be seen."

"I have no interest in being some macho douchebag like you! And don't say 'meager'! After that FPS match with Izuna, I realized my physical fitness is actually important and started working out a little, believe it or not!"

His venom spent, Sora clucked his tongue once in irritation and lay back down.

He kept silent about how he himself had been surprised that his limit for crunches and push-ups was fifty.

"…Anyway, screw you. Where's everyone else?"

"Women take time to get ready, Sir—pardon me, is this news to you?"

"I'm trying to say I hate sitting here talking to a macho old fart! Have you heard of sarcasm?! Have you?!"

Squinting and yelling, Sora turned his gaze behind him.

"Yooo, Shirooo, are you done yeeet?"

"…Mm, just…a little longer…"

Shiro's voice emerged from the trees at Sora's back. There was some rustling or something going on back there, but in any case, it seemed she was having trouble changing by herself.

"What would be the problem with simply changing in the changing room with the other ladies?"

"You said it. In fact, that's just what I said, until I got chased the hell out…*by you!*"

Sora and Shiro could not separate. Changing was no exception. Under this self-evident truth, at his usual pace, as nature would have it, in the most natural way, Sora had attempted to follow Shiro into the girls' changing room—then got chased the hell out, and here we were.

"Let you peep on the bare flesh of the Holy Shrine Maiden? Even if Tet forgives it, I never will."

"Dude, the Shrine Maiden was all, ''Tis no matter to meee'—!"

Suddenly a sense of humiliation overcame him for having bowed to the intimidation of a muscled old fart in a loincloth.

—Was it too late to rush past Ino? Sora painted the plot in his mind, yet—

"…Here you bitches go, please."

"Hmmm…Izuna, my dear, you're so darling no matter what you wear!"

At the the young girl's salutation and the sudden transformation of Ino's voice into that of a sweet old man, Sora turned. Izuna was the first to show up fully changed, and Ino softly sighed, laying a hand on his chest.

"When I heard *the swimsuits were chosen by Sora*—I was worried at what sort of disgrace might be forced upon you."

"You ignorant old fart! For starters, everyone knows a little girl is supposed to wear a school swimsuit!"

Izuna toddled down the sand, waving her big tail. Her swimsuit was from Sora and Shiro's world...an old-school swimsuit. Naturally, until now, such a thing had not existed in this world. It should also be noted that synthetic fibers such as polyester were not available, even in the Eastern Union. However, school swimsuits originally, before the war, had been made of silk. Using the disturbingly detailed information recorded in the tablet, Steph had recreated the garb most admirably. Steph—the highest of props to you.

"...But you really did manage to keep it quite modest."

"Once more I tell you: Old fart, you are ignorant. What sort of romanticism is there to be had without taking culture into account?!"

—Yes, Izuna, on top of her school swimsuit, wore a jacket-like garment with dangling sleeves and an open front like those of the surrounding Werebeasts. Animal ears. Little girl. School swimsuit. All fused with the culture of the Eastern Union—!

—This—

—was Sora's—"answer"...

Standing before Sora, Izuna spun around as if looking behind her.

"Is this okay, please?"

"*C'est magnifique*... You were already so cute it's not even fair, and now you're a frickin' cultural heritage."

Ino watched Sora flash a thumbs-up and a fine-young-man smile.

"...I can't say I follow, but you have my honest praise for not seeking lasciviousness in my granddaughter."

—Then.

"U-umm...I-I'm done changing."

"Oh, Steph. Wowww, you did some fine work——"

Turning toward Steph's shy voice to commend her—Sora froze. The red-faced Steph had preserved the lacey, girly image of her normal clothes as she wore a bikini-style swimsuit decked out in frills and a pareo, squirming and shifting her eyes as if she didn't know what to do. As far as Sora knew, Elkia had no swimsuits like that. In Elkia, a swimsuit meant—you know. Those full-body drawers that passed for swimsuits in the dark ages of seventeenth-century Europe. That was why he had asked Steph to make some proper swimwear. From the look on her face, it could be surmised that Steph had conformed to the swimsuit design Sora and Shiro had ordered for her as well. Sora froze like a rock—but not for the bikini. Rather, it was the ample volumes that threatened to spill from its top that stunned him, sending figures bounding through his brain.

"—It—it can't be. Eighty-nine, fifty-eight, eighty-nine...a power level of fifty thousand—?!"

"H-how did you—? I mean, no! What are you talking about?!"

Sora shivered at the unexpected boob force indicated by the meter in his brain. What could explain this? Had he all this time overlooked it as a consequence of the undue diligence of Mr. Steam?!

"...Mm, mmgh... How can Steph be so high-level——?!"

"Er, uh, I—am I? I-I wouldn't say that..."

Steph squirmed as if not entirely displeased. Sora opened his mouth to utter another word or two—but was stopped short.

"Please excuse me, Master. It took some time to 'weave' the appearance you requested."

"Heh-heh-heh, you mustn't worry, dearie. Keeping a lad biting his nails while waiting is what a good woman does, don't you know?"

At the two voices, everyone turned—and in that instant, the needle on the meter in Sora's brain was pinned at maximum. Sora and Ino, before they could think, followed their instincts. Which told them it was their duty to throw themselves on the ground then and there. Where they'd turned were—indeed—two goddesses.

Two goddesses—of whom one was Jibril. Her long hair, which reflected light and changed color, fanned by the breeze in the seaside

sunlight, grew all the more brilliant. A sculpted beauty, worthy of being called the ultimate, at which any sculptor's heart would break at first glance. Covering this masterpiece of a body was the swimsuit Sora had specified. For Jibril, who showed plenty of skin regularly, he'd intentionally picked a one-piece, woven with string across her midsection. From a largish shawl wrapped like a pareo around her hips extended her faintly glistening wings. The halo turning above her head took all this divine splendor and made it still greater. Her beauty was such that it stole away any room for doubt she'd come from the sky, rendering the reality beyond question.

Two goddesses—of whom one was the Shrine Maiden. Her golden hair and ears and tails, and her fair skin, lit by the sunlight, could only be summarized as—an aureole.

Lines somewhat more reserved, but if Jibril was the ultimate—the Shrine Maiden could only be the supreme. Her soft skin, usually wrapped in a kimono, was now wreathed in the consistent theme of a swimsuit resembling a short Japanese-style jacket. But through her languid manner of dress suggestive of a club hostess, a "butter-fly of the night," her shoulders peeped lithely, lustrous. Her golden hair and two tails, scintillating as they slowly waved with each step on the sand, and the bewitching smile that arose on her face, con-vinced one of the existence of the fox spirits that were said to live forever and ascend to the divine—no mere spirit, but a deity who stood above them all. Tears streamed down the faces of the two earthbound men. They did not know why, yet without understand-ing anything, they prayed.

"...I, Ino Hatsuse, have finally learned the reason I was borrrn—!"

"Ohhh, god! I don't know who or where you are, but, friggin' inspired god who created Jibril and the Shrine Maiden for us in this world—ahh, make me your disciple..."

A new religion was rising up. Steph and Izuna, having witnessed one of its key tenets, felt obliged to interject.

"—Excuse me. I recognize that it's a hard comparison to stand up to...but can you really treat us this differently?"

"...? Didja all get sand in your eyes, please?"

Izuna, looking back and forth between Steph and the two still prostrate, looked puzzled.

"Oh, Master, you honor me more than I deserve, but please raise your head!!"

"Hmp, don't stand on ceremony, lads. You may as well savor the blessing of my seaside attire!"

Jibril lowered her head to the ground at the sight of Sora's state as the Shrine Maiden crowed with laughter. At the women's urging, Sora and Ino rose tentatively. Faced again with the divine radiance of the two, Sora and Ino turned their gazes toward the sky together.

"...Somehow, it feels like I've already experienced more than enough."

"...I must concur. My heart fills with the feeling that I have done my bit."

"...Shall we go back now?"

"...For once, our opinions coincide, Sir."

—Apparently it was philosophy time for the two men. Though ever at odds, in this setting alone, there was no bad blood, no wall between the races. The two simply, as fellow men, looked up to the sky together and nodded with the same feeling in their hearts.

—Why must there be fighting? When the world is so very beautiful—

"Hey, hold on there! What do you suppose you came here for?!"

Upon the two walking the path of enlightenment, Steph's voice rang down like a clarion.

—What indeed.

"...Why was it again?"

"I am afraid, Master, that by my recollection, it was to visit the city of Siren."

...Oh, that's right. Sora finally remembered.

—Indeed. As Jibril had said, they hadn't come just to swim. They'd come because Plum had indicated that a boat from Siren would arrive to pick them up. After all, the city of Siren—Oceand—was at the bottom of the sea. Jibril, neither having visited nor able to see it, was unable to shift there. Thus, Plum was to be their guide, but—

"So where the hell is Plum?"

"I-I'm here..."

"Whoa?!"

Sora jumped at the little voice coming from his feet. How long had she been there? Almost imperceptibly, two eyes peeked out of a crate by his feet.

"...Uh, is that you, Plum? The hell are you doing? This is the beach."

"P-please don't be unreasonablle... Th-this is the most I can dooo?"

Plum answered, producing one of the patterns that arose when she used magic—and tears while she was at it.

"Master, direct sunlight is lethal to Dhampir. Even with that box around her, she must bend light or she will—"

At Jibril's words, Sora remembered the "illness." So given that it was *transmitted* by sucking blood, that meant that the Dhampir *herself* couldn't get out in the sun?

"The greeting vessel from Oceand is to come at *night*, you knowww? Why are we here in the middle of the day...?"

—Indeed. The boat was supposed to pick them up after the sun set. Plum, groaning, *Why did we have to come here when the daylight is like the flames of hell—?*

"But d00d, it's the beach. You want me to skip past the swimsuit scene when we've got this crew? Are you nuts?"

—Though even Sora would have excused himself if he didn't have Jibril's mysterious sunscreen.

"Hey, come to think of it, Jibril. Won't that sunscreen work on Plum?"

"Unfortunately, Master, for Dhampirs, it is being exposed to the sun *itself* that is lethal."

At Jibril's unqualified ruling-out of hope, Plum provided a correction.

"Uh, no… If I weave a more powerful rite, I'll be fiiine…but, you know, it'll use a lot of power…"

Considering how tired she'd looked when she had first come to them, basically she was saying that walking straight through this blazing sun would wear her out to that point.

"Y-you seee…Sirens' blood just isn't enough to, uh, d-do anything biiig…so."

Whooosh, Plum peeked out of the box with a nice smile.

"If I could! Just lick the feet of Queen Shiro one more time, I'll have no trouble with that riiite…eh-heh-hehh!"

"Denied. You just squat there."

At the swift stroke that cleft her proposal in twain, Plum let out only a moan as she plonked her crate closed again.

"…Hey, for being Rank Twelve, isn't Plum just too frickin' weak?"

—This was something he'd always thought about the vampires postulated in his own world, but still…

"Dhampirs amplify their power with the blood they intake—the strength of its soul," Jibril answered. "If they ingest blood befitting the height of their natural aptitude for illusion and stealth—for instance, the blood of Elf—they become the vilest of assassins. In the Great War, they were, in fact, something of a threat."

…*Ah*, Sora thought, remembering that first night. Allowing that she was off her guard, even Jibril had fallen prey to Plum's tricks for a time—but.

"—Now look at them, right…"

Sora mumbled, squinting down at the crate as his feet. Seeing that she was still trembling even inside the crate was almost sufficient to bring tears to one's eyes.

"—I've been thinking this for a while, but aren't Elf and Flügel a little too different in power for being just one rank apart? I mean, you're saying this twerp can drink Elf's blood, but she's gonna vaporize if she drinks yours, right?"

Sora indicated the crate at his feet as he posed the question.

"Yes, for that is just where the 'separation line' lies in the ranking," said Jibril.

"'Separation line'?"

"Simply speaking, ranks up to Seven are 'living things,' whereas higher ranks are 'living beings.'"

"...Huh?"

"You might understand it best by thinking of ranks up to Seven as those possessing physical bodies, who reproduce by ordinary means, and are generally defined as 'living things,' whereas the higher ranks are energies or concepts that have acquired will, or in other words 'living beings.'"

—Hmm, then it was simple. It was *the line at which common sense no longer applied.* Sora understood.

"While we're on the subject, what about one above you, Jibril—Gigant, was it? What's the power relationship look like with those guys?"

"...Well you might ask. I should say a single standard Gigant might be a feat to slay alone. If we aim for certainty, I should desire five companions. What, there are plans to slay one? ♥"

"No, there aren't. Stop sparkling your eyes!"

The dejected Jibril could destroy Elf, highest of the "living things," alone, with a single blow. But it would take a party of six like her to bring down one individual of Rank Five.

—The races Rank Seven and below, you could say, did a pretty good job surviving the Great War. Especially Immanity, I mean, us—that is.

"Speaking of us... Heyyy, Shiro, aren't you done changing yet?"

Suddenly remembering that she was taking quite the long time, Sora called into the trees behind him.

"......Mm."

In response to Sora's voice, Shiro poked just her face out from the shade of a tree. Sora realized she seemed hesitant to come out for some reason.

"What's wrong, Shiro? You can't stand the sun after all? You don't have to if it's too tough, you know."

Though he'd put on Jibril-brand sunscreen, Sora himself was not fond of sunlight. On top of that, Sora knew Shiro hated sunlight even more than he did—and thus sympathized. But then Shiro shook her head from side to side and finally, hesitantly, stepped out from the trees.

"...Hmm, well, that is something."

"Dearie me, if you aren't the cutest little one."

"...Shiro, you're damn pretty, please."

As Ino, the Shrine Maiden, and Izuna each dropped their individual comments—Sora was simply frozen. Standing there was, clearly, the same sister he'd always seen.

—The same—and yet.

"—...Huh?"

As she tremulously left the shade of the trees, the girl was like a jewel. Her long hair, whiter than snow at normal times, had been combed out neatly and tied at the back. Illuminated by the sunlight, it was no longer like snow—but a petrifact, a diamond. From her white bikini and red hoodie, which seemed to symbolize her hair and ruby eyes, peeked her skin—

"......Bro-ther...?"

—which, just like her cheeks, carried a faint vermilion flush.

"—Wh-what? Uh?"

At the unnatural feeling of having been completely entranced by his sister, a questioning groan escaped Sora's lips. But at that groan, Shiro's face clouded with worry.

"...I, don't...look good, after all...?"

As Shiro mumbled with her eyes lowered and receded back toward the trees, Sora finally came back to his senses. In a panic—to the extent that he himself wondered what he was getting so flustered about—he shook his head.

"N-no, that's not it!! I was just amazed at what an unbelievable beauty you are, Shiro—I mean, y-you know your brother already knew you're a flawless beauty! I already...knew, right? What?"

Shiro disregarded Sora as he tilted his head wondering what had surprised him so much. At his side, Jibril and Steph, likewise entranced, beamed. Their expressions betrayed their hearts leaping in their chests.

—Shiro cast her gaze downward shyly and, almost invisibly, smiled in relief.

"Oh. That's...good..."

......

"Indeed my master is wise... It is a feast of which my eyes are unworthy. ♥"

"It's not like that! It's not like that! It's quite normal to react to cute things, I sayyyy!"

Her skin glistening, Jibril smoothly sighed, *Hff...* While Steph again clenched her head as if in some kind of turmoil.

"...Brother...?"

"Y-yeah? Mm, hmm, you look great! That's my darling sister!"

Reacting to Shiro who'd walked up to him, Sora struggling to regain his composure. Shiro, her hair mussed by her brother, nodded once as if finally satisfied.

"—Th-that's right, Plum, when specifically is your welcoming party or whatever coming?"

Sora, feeling awkward somehow and then remembering his original purpose, questioned the Dhampir. At Sora's words, everyone turned their eyes to the crate—to Plum.

Her face emerging slightly from the crate, Plum responded.

"Umm, around when the date changes...they'll arriiive."

"—Hmph, that's quite a long time."

Disbelievingly, Plum grumbled. "That's why I said you didn't have to come this earlyyy…mghhh." She said only this—perhaps unable to bear the sunlight—before retreating into her crate once more.

"Well, 'tis no real loss, is it?" Thus brushing off any inconvenience, the Shrine Maiden answered elegantly, at some point having rolled onto the grassy bed upon which Sora had been reclining, as she was fanned with giant leaves by her servant girls. "Why not think it a long-deserved holiday and rest your bones as you wait. What is life without a bit of leisure?"

Grinning and scratching his head, Sora exchanged glances with Shiro. Shiro nodded once.

"Now that I think about it, this is the first time Shiro and I have ever been to the beach."

Then, looking around at the eyes of Steph, Jibril, Izuna, and Ino, Sora smiled.

"Why don't we give this *fun* thing a try?"

■■■

—A blinding white beach. A sea that reflected the sky like a mirror. Through a sky so blue it looked like nothing so much as a primary-color ink spill, the rays of sun spilled down, and the distant clouds flowed. In a place where the only noise was that of the rippling waves and the roar of the sea, sprays of mist soared through the air. It was here, at a party, frolicking in the shallow water wetting her legs, that Shiro served a fabric beach ball.

"…Steph… Pass."

"I just have to bounce it on, yes? Here, pass, Miss Izuna!"

Steph deftly set the pass from Shiro high in the air toward Izuna. However, Izuna simply caught the ball as it flew toward her: *Fump.*

"…? I don't get the damn rules, please," she muttered in bewilderment, her head tilted. Unlike Steph, who'd gotten the idea, it seemed Izuna didn't grasp the point.

"Uhh, it's not really a *game*, is the thing... Well, okay, let's say this. You can't grab the ball. You have to pass the ball to the next person only touching it once, and if you can't, then you *lose*—right?"

"...Understood, please..."

Watching Izuna's nod with a warm and fuzzy look, Steph rambled, blissfully ignorant. "How nice... It's wonderful to play a game like this where we can just relax once in a while, isn't it?"

Yes, blissfully ignorant of the fact that Sora's and Shiro's eyes, as well as Izuna's, had sharpened to the keenness of blades. As soon as rules had been set out and explicated, what we had here—was a game, pure and simple.

—Which meant—

—*I'll, kick your ass*—! The three other than the maudlin Steph thus bared their fighting spirits entirely openly...

"...'Kay, then...I'll, go, first..."

With these words, Shiro, having been given the ball, quietly exchanged glances with Sora.

—Shiro took the ball and casually dipped it in the water.

"...Here...Steph, pass..."

And so the *fabric* beach ball, with only its bottom wet, was tossed to Steph without spin. And to be clear—*in the precise moment there was no wind.*

"Yes, yes, passing it ooon!"

Silent diplomacy streaked through the air, but Steph set for the return without recognizing this. The ball that Shiro had sent rigged—if Steph set it without moving—*to go slightly off course.* As a result, the ball passed by Steph to Izuna had spin.

—But weighed down by the water absorbed just at its bottom, the ball's course swayed irregularly.

"——!"

Izuna, however, read this instantly. Launching off the ground in a spray of water, she caught up with the ball and received it. Only received it. By the measure of Izuna's arms, it was a light return. But through Izuna's little body, the ball had acquired the overwhelming force of Werebeast.

—That was enough to send it hurtling at Sora with terrifying speed. But Sora, seemingly unfazed by this, thought to himself: *Well, hope you don't think it's gonna be that easy!* In the trajectory of the ball that had been only received by Izuna but was nonetheless flying at him as if spiked by a pro volleyball player, Sora intentionally fell dramatically into the water, raising an aqueous pillar. The projectile penetrated the pillar, but by the time it reached the collapsed Sora, its speed was negligible. From this unreasonable position, Sora somehow set the ball with his feet and sent it over to Shiro.

—*Now thoroughly soaked, the ball had gotten quite heavy.*

"...Mm—Steph...go, for it..."

Shiro just barely managed to set up the wet and abruptly heavier ball for Steph.

"Uh, h-huh?!"

Yes—*with incomparable precision* to a point Steph *could just barely reach.* To a position from which, even if she got it given the angles of entry and escape, Steph—

"Uh, I'm sorry, Miss Izu—"

—managing to keep it in play, inevitably sent it careening a considerable distance from Izuna.

—She couldn't get it. With the ball flying off in some totally wrong direction, there was no way she could reach, yet—

—At Sora and Shiro, subtly raising the corners of their mouths as if to say *and that's the game*, Izuna ground her teeth.

"...Don't screw with me—please!!!"

She launched off the ground. She landed—*impact*. The water that had been at her feet now explosively scattered to reveal the sand beneath at the shock of her step—but flying as if to outstrip it, as if gliding over the ocean, Izuna caught up to the ball and, still at that speed, swung her arms. The shock wave of her swing was enough to raise a wave—but—

Powww—

Water sprayed as a fine mist from within the ball, which exploded in Izuna's hands. Sora raised his voice.

"GG, you lose!"

"—?...! Th-that's not fair, please! You bastards, please!"

"If you don't pass it on to the next person, you lose...Izzy... Using, all your strength, was your downfall." Shiro answered, exchanging a light high-five with Sora.

That's right: if Izuna, a Werebeast, hit the ball, heavy with water, *with all her might*, at that moment, the ball, unable to bear the shock, would rupture, and she'd be unable to pass it on to the next person. Once she realized that had been Sora and Shiro's aim all along, Izuna still argued.

—But what if the ball hadn't ruptured then? "...You people... Don't you even have the concept of playing just for fun?" Steph muttered, doused by the wave produced by Izuna's step and subsequent swing...

"Huh? Not for *games*, nope."

"...Lol...wut?"

"Isn't the damn point of games to kick ass, please?"

At the three immediate answers, each incredibly immature in its own way, Steph gave herself over to the wave—

Meanwhile, the Shrine Maiden, who had been watching from a distance, spoke up in wonder.

"Well!...You beat Izuna at sports. 'Tis a feat, aye... Your disregard for the spirit of the rules is as remarkable as ever, but even so, I must——?!"

—Her words broke off. At the instant sensation of someone behind her, the Shrine Maiden promptly moved her hands to her chest. But however unhinged Werebeast's reaction times may have been, the blink of an eye wasn't fast enough. Having suddenly had her swimsuit pilfered, the Shrine Maiden did the best she could to hide her breasts as she directed a sharp glare at the culprit.

"—Goodness, just what are you after, my dear *pigeon*!"

Jibril received the look while playing with the swimsuit she had stripped from the Shrine Maiden.

"According to my masters' literature, in a situation such as this, a 'nip slip' is the *law of fate*!"

"Ohh, I see... In which case, we can of course expect you to fulfill this fate, eh? ♥"

Still hiding her chest, the Shrine Maiden softly lowered her center of gravity. As the Shrine Maiden unmistakably assumed a fighting posture, Jibril only laughed at her merrily.

"Indeed, to this I object not. However, if you suppose that a little dog with no power but to crawl the earth is capable of taking anything from me—I must suggest that you reconsider your position. ♥"

"Heh-heh! ♪ You talk, don't you? But you've got it wrong. I've got more powers than crawling the earth. ♫"

Still smiling, but with sparks of hostility flying so fiercely it seemed you could see them—

——......

"Oh, Shiro, you don't know how to swim?"

"...Huh, Steph...you, can?"

Steph balked at this new revelation about Shiro, who had seemed capable of anything. But with Shiro gawking at someone who could swim—

"...Holy shit, please."

"No less should be expected of Miss Stephanie. From administration to cuisine to needlecraft... And then to think you can swim. But, if I may ask innocently—for what reason is it necessary for animals that live on land to be able to swim in water?!"

"Gramps just made the point of the century! Land animals should live on land!!"

—The whole crew, apparently bereft of anyone who could swim, spoke as one. Steph, with a wry smile, took Shiro's hands.

"You're all hopeless. It's more fun if you can swim. Here, I shall teach you."

"...Mnghhh..."

"Come now, I have your hands; let's try kicking to start."

Drawing Shiro by her hands, Steph soothed the unenthusiastic girl and tried to teach her the basics.

—But—

"Whoaaaaaa!"

"Eeyaaaaaaaaaaaaaahhhh!"

Suddenly, a massive wave arose and carried them all straight to shore.

"...Uwp...ah...B-Brother..."

"Wauugh, Shiroooo!"

Shiro swept to shore by the wave, Sora ran in a panic and lifted her up. Hugging her panting brother, Shiro muttered.

"...Brother...I'm, gonna, learn...to swiiim!"

But faced with Shiro, as if the seawater had gotten to her, mumbling this determination with tears in her eyes, Sora confronted those responsible for the massive wave, raising his voice.

"Hey there! Maybe you should consider moderating—I mean, at least obeying the laws of physics...if you don't mind?"

The voice he'd raised, though, trailed off at the sight before his eyes. That sight being: crisscrossing the distant horizons of the sea, two...monsters.

"Hee-hee, though your words be grand, this is all we could ever expect, isn't it, isn't it? ♥"

Jibril taunted this as she cut across the water. Just below her, the body of the Shrine Maiden, leaping from the ocean floor, turned scarlet as she stretched out her hand.

—The hand of the Shrine Maiden, who'd gone so far as to use her bloodbreak, was nevertheless dodged by Jabril by the slimmest of margins. But the Shrine Maiden went on—bounding and dashing over the surface of the water—**using her hands as a bra**. The Shrine Maiden, apparently having lost not only her swimsuit top, but now even her *hanten*, had become so overwhelmed with something akin to a murderous rage that she'd lost the will to hide and was pursuing Jibril to get her swimsuit back.

"Heh-heh-heh! If I were you, I say, I'd prepare for the worrrst... I'll strip you to your bum in front of eeeveryone!"

The Shrine Maiden. The agent plenipotentiary of Werebeast—the strongest among Werebeast, was she? Running atop the water—on the water!—and sometimes, albeit just for a moment, *even on the air*. The Shrine Maiden, dunking herself again and again in the sea, bathing in the water and wind, changing in appearance each time from scarlet to gold—

"...Th-that's...our Holy Shrine Maiden, holy shit, please."

—but the one thing that was certain, as even Izuna watched in disbelief, was that no one could intervene. Sora decided to write it off as a natural calamity and looked away.

"Hmm... What a fine sight."

At these words, Sora turned to see Ino, and he followed the old man's gaze to find not only those who had been swept to shore—Steph and Izuna—but also, sopping wet from the wave that had clearly soaked the entire beach, the Shrine Maiden's servant girls. Huddled together as if their swimsuits were suddenly transparent, they presented a vision that transcended words.

"Huh... All right, then. It's still unforgivable to nearly drown Shiro, but this is *marvelous*," Sora commented, returning to the beach with Shiro still in his arms.

"Yeees, a feast for the eyes, is it not, Your Majesty?"

"Yeah, if we just didn't have you here, it woulda been perfect."

This Sora muttered to the muscular old man who wore nothing but a loincloth, doing his level best to keep the geezer out of his line of sight.

Watching everyone frolicking, caressed by the waves, Steph smiled warmly.

"Hee-hee... We've been working so hard for so long..."

The brilliant rays of sunshine, the white sand. Returning to the tide, she lightly kicked at the water, *splish, splash.* The waves lapping at her feet, the wind blowing from the ocean, as if chasing away her daily toils—

"...Everyone needs a break now and then, don't they?"

Steph whispered with a deep sense of relief. At the pleasant scent of the salty air, she wondered to herself when had been the last time that she had taken it easy like this? It must have been before Sora and Shiro came—no, before her grandfather passed away. Feeling that she had not released her tension for many years—she took a deep breath.

"I'm so glad we came...!" Steph declared, seeking assent from no one in particular.

————Bee-bee-bee-bee-beep

"That's a wrap! Good work, everyoooone!!"

As Sora thus called with half-open eyes...*shuffle, shuffle*...they came like zombies, trudging back from the sea.

"...Nghh... My hair, is all stiff...full of, sand..."

"Hff...I do apologize, Master, but I simply cannot bring myself to find an affinity for the sea... The salt breeze gets in my wings, and I know not what to say of the discomfort."

"My tail sucks up the water and gets all heavy, please... It's a pain in the ass, please."

"Hff, enough is *quite* enough if you ask me. Who came up with this baffling ceremony of bathing in the sea?"

"O Holy Shrine Maiden, I apologize. I should not have allowed you to become involved in this farce of King Sora's."

Despite the troupe's sudden transformation, not unlike actors having just finished a performance, there was one member—

"...Huh? Wh-what?"

—unable to follow. Steph, watching dazedly, stood alone in the sea.

"—Mm? What are you doing, Steph? We got the footage. It's fine. You can come out now."

Sora said this while disabling his phone and tablet, which were mounted on beachside trees.

"...Huh? What? What do you mean?"

"—Mm? Huh, you mean you were actually enjoying it for real?"

Having moved into the shade to towel themselves off, everyone looked confused.

"...Uhh, sorry. Let's see now, Steph... The truth is..."

Sora, apparently certain she had been aware the whole time, spoke as if reluctant to say it.

"...No one here actually likes the beach..."

—...Mm-hmm... A large, deep collective nod from the group. The Shrine Maiden, who seemed the most uncomfortable of all of them, spoke as she groomed her golden fur.

"I gave this 'trope' Mr. Sora spoke of a whirl...but it's still a mystery to me... With all this sand in my tail... How do you reckon I shall get this out?"

"Lord Shiro—it is time!"

Jibril, her eyes flashing, handed something to Shiro.

—*Props* was the response indicated by Shiro's thumb, her eyes gleaming the same.

"...Shrine, Maiden...you should, try...this brush, and this, shampoo."

"Oh, is that so? Well, let's give it a try, then."

"…Fluffy, fluffy…hee-hee…"

Shiro, having deftly gained an excuse to fulfill her desires, smiled darkly as she buried her face in the Shrine Maiden's golden tail. And, before you knew it, Sora was at it, too, with the same contents in his hands.

"Yayyy-yooo, now I'm gonna do Izuna's—"

But Ino towered in the young man's path. Looks were exchanged in an instant—two men face-to-face. "I shall tend to Izuna. Here, here, Izuna, this way."

"…Gramps, why don't you take care of your own damn tail?"

"To be groomed by you, Sir, would defile Izuna. Why do you not do something about that meager body of your own?"

But, paying no attention to these two, Izuna toddled straight *in front of Ino*, and plopped down.

"Get this shit done, please."

"…………………………………………………"

"…Old fart, that thing you're doing with your face makes me want to kill you without you saying anything. Is that some kind of special Werebeast power?"

In response to Ino's expression, which seemed moments away from audibly echoing with a sound like *owwnnnned*, a vein bulged on Sora's forehead.

…*Fshh*, a wave splashed over Steph's legs.

—It seemed the time when anyone had been aware of her had come and gone…

■■■

—The sun was creeping below the horizon.

"…Hee-hee, it's so beautiful…hee-hee-hee…"

Sitting with her arms around her knees on the beach, Steph, having apparently fled into her own little world…was smiling.

—Then suddenly Sora spoke.

* * *

"———I'm bored."

At this one phrase, the gazes of all collected on Sora.

"Hng, only bastards quit while they're ahead, please."

Izuna expressed her discontentment at Sora's words; Sora, who had been whiling away all this time until sunset with Izuna and his DSP, *shogi*, tic-tac-toe, and other distractions that made one question why they'd bothered to come to the beach in the first place.

"Uhh, no, I didn't mean I'm bored of playing games with you."

Rising, Sora addressed the nearby crate.

"Hey, Plum, where's your welcome boat?"

""Ah!""

——Voices rose at this reminder of their original purpose, which almost everyone had forgotten, and Plum meekly poked her face out of the crate. Plum—who must have been working her magic the whole time judging from her face, which was so exhausted as to harken back to their first meeting—answered:

"Nghh, I—I told youuu, it's coming around when the date changes, didn't I...?"

"But, I mean, my DSP and tablet are practically outta batteries. I'm pretty much done here."

"That's why I told you we didn't need to come so earlyyy..."

Nghh... Plum whined, her exhaustion clouded with dissatisfaction.

"Nooo, I'm bored. I wanna go now. Otherwise I'm going home," Sora said like a spoiled child.

"How can you be so childiiish...?"

Sora ignored the petulant Plum and exchanged glances with the Shrine Maiden and Shiro. The Shrine Maiden—who since getting out of the water had been thoroughly fluffed up in the shade by Shiro—and Shiro, who had been doing the fluffing.

—Both nodded subtly and muttered together.

"Right you are, lad...I must say this is getting tiresome."

"...Mm...I'm...tired, too..."

"Whaa... You, too? How can you be so...?"

Ignoring Plum, who seemed consumed by sorrow, Sora opened his mouth.

"Jibril."

"I am here." Jibril materialized from the void at the first mention of her name.

"Have you pinned down the location?"

"Yes, Master. I believe that the location you and Lord Shiro calculated is accurate."

—*Calculated?* Sora took out his tablet for Plum, who didn't seem to understand what this was about. On the map of the plots of neighboring areas of the Eastern Union was displayed a rough estimate of the position of the city, which Shiro had traced back from such factors as the slight amount of trade conducted by Oceand. Looking over to the real-world position—beyond the horizon—Sora spoke.

"All right, I guess we're ready—*do it.*"

"——Your wish is my command!"

At Sora's words, loosening her expression into a joy she could not conceal, Jibril knelt and executed his order.

"Huh, wh-what are you going to dooo...?"

Plum nervously voiced the same question Ino wanted to ask. Ino's Werebeast intuition was blaring an alarm. *Identify it. As circumstances require, stop it. These bastards are up to no good.* So Ino glanced at the Shrine Maiden. Seeing her slowly nod, *No problem,* he sighed in relief. But then—at the Shrine Maiden's snide expression adding, *But watch out,* Ino went pale. Sora lifted Shiro and offhandedly announced:

"*We're bustin' in.* Everyone get back."

As the two edged away from the beach, Jibril turned to Sora and Shiro.

"——Master, are you certain it's all right?" As if unable to wait, yet, for form's sake, squirming, she sought final confirmation.

"Sure. In any case, it's gonna be constrained by the Ten Covenants, right?"

The First of the Ten Covenants.

—In this world, all force of arms and bodily injury are forbidden.

"Any action that's considered to be malicious or an exercise of force of arms is canceled by the binding power of the Covenants— looked at the other way, *actions without malice are not canceled.* Which means that, if an action is executed, that means 'Lord Tet' himself has put down his seal of approval saying it doesn't violate anyone's rights—so."

With these words, Sora raised his thumb with a bold smile.

"Do what you can do for the win."

At this reply, a solemn bow as if receiving the word of heaven. But, contrastingly, making a sloppy smile, Jibril stood.

"Eh-heh, eh-heh-heh-hehh, how many years has it been? Geh-heh-hehh, I cannot waiiit…"

As Jibril whispered with a drunken expression, her surroundings suddenly distorted. Clearly light—no, *space*—seemed to wrench and warp.

—The Ten Covenants. This was a world in which the exercise of force of arms and bodily injury was forbidden by absolutely binding Covenants. Ino supposedly understood it more than well enough, yet the scene made his skin crawl.

"Come now, all fall back!" came the calm yet sharp voice of the Shrine Maiden. At this brief command, without connection to their consciousness, all the Werebeasts there reflexively jumped far away.

"…Huh? What is going on?" Steph was finally brought back to the real world by the Shrine Maiden's shout.

She realized that she was the only one still so close to the sea.

Thunk—space quivered with a sound outside the audible range. Warped farther as even the sand on the beach was made to forget about gravity and float into the air. Bending and twisting, space converged in Jibril's hand. The only one there who could see magic—spirits—Plum. Yet she watched utterly at a loss as to what Jibril was trying to do. If it was as Sora had been told before…it was *only natural*. What Jibril was doing—was squeezing all the spirits out of their surroundings. If there were no spirits to see, nothing could be seen. It was much like a black hole. And—in Jibril's palm, the wrung-out spirits were compacted, compressed, condensed, contracted, concentrated, and at last began emitting light. It shone clearly even to the eyes of Sora and Shiro, Immanities incapable of seeing spirits. In Jibril's right hand, a column of light that seemed to whirl began to form. Sora and Shiro were fundamentally unable to grasp or detect the likes of magic or spirits—and yet. The halo above Jibril's head was spinning so fast it was already just a blur. There was only one thing this could mean—

"…Hey, uh, y-you can't be seriouuus! Wh-whaa, you meaaan—?!"

Finally grasping the situation, Plum scrambled to take cover, but, unable to escape from her crate, she just screamed. Yes, there was only one thing this spectacle could mean. It was something the likes of which, at the very least, Sora and Shiro had never seen. Jibril was about to exercise magic on a level that defied conventional expectations.

Jibril's right hand gripped *it* firmly, though it was too amorphous to be called a sword or spear. And—slowly raising *it* above her head—she smiled sunnily.

"Very well, Master.

"I shall proceed—with about five percent of my full power. ♥"

At a speed that left these words far behind, Jibril's right arm swung down. That was as much as Sora and Shiro were able to see. With a lag like that between the sight of distant lightning and the sound of the following thunder, a few moments later roared a boom that shook the earth as waves reached almost to the heavens and—almost like some kind of joke—the sea parted. Then—

"Eeyaaaaaaaaaaaaaaaaaah!"

"Aaaaaauuuuuuuughhhh—"

In the wake of the tempestuous impact, Steph—as well as Plum, still in her crate—rolled to Shiro's and Sora's feet.

—That was everything they were able to perceive next.

"Hff...♥ It is such a delight to be able to put forth force." Jibril bared a huge, refreshed smile. "I can only pray to one day be blessed again with a chance to put forth my all—one hundred percent. ♥"

But at these words even Sora and Shiro broke into a cold sweat. Even Moses would be incredulous at how cleanly she had parted the sea...and then they remembered that Jibril had once unleashed her full power on Elf, that is, 100 percent, with her "Heavenly Smite." And, albeit not entirely, they had managed to defend themselves *somewhat*—

"...Elf...Fiel's guys are pretty sick."

"...Nod, nod."

At Sora's involuntary acknowledgment of their crew currently in absentia, Shiro nodded.

Jibril, though, was unable to know what lay in their hearts. "With this I have succeeded in seeing the city of Siren. We may shift there at any time."

...The Werebeasts' senses approached physical limits, but of course, Ino and Izuna and even the Shrine Maiden were incapable of seeing anything but the horizon. At this point, no one could say a word to Jibril, claiming she'd seen it as if she'd bent light itself with that blow of hers.

—Sora looked around at the wide berth that had been cleared around the Flügel.

"'Kay, guys, let's go. Grab onto Jibril."

The appalled Shrine Maiden returned gingerly to the beach with the Werebeasts.

"I thought myself aware of it...but, seen in the flesh, that is one cruel joke."

"...Nghhh... If you can help it, you really shouldn't get involved with Flügel at allll..." Crawling out of her broken crate, Plum concurred. Fortunately for her, the sun had already set.

Ino suddenly raised his voice in a panic. "Sir! Will you please not subject our Holy Shrine Maiden to that sound!"

In apparent terror of the sound from the distortion of space in a long-distance shift, Ino was roaring.

"Oh, yeah. Jibril."

"Yes, I understand the situation. With that—everyone please take hold...oh, please, Dora, if you'll just interrupt your nap for a moment and come here."

"...Uh, huh? What's going—wh-what is this?! The sea has parteeeed?!"

Everyone gathered around Jibril, ignoring Steph and her lonely shrieking.

"And now we shall shift to the metropolis of Siren—Oceand."

Once more, Jibril's wings started to glow, and again her halo increased its RPM.

"The distance is 378.23 kilometers; however, the parted sea will return any second now."

As if responding to her words, the sea closed up with a roar.

"Therefore, it is surmised that Oceand lacks air."

"Oh, d-don't worryyy; I've got a spell for breathing—"

But, whether she didn't hear Plum's voice or simply ignored it—

"Therefore—I will shift us along with all the air in a two-hundred-meter radius!"

"—Hungh?"

"Fall back!"

The Shrine Maiden's voice rang out once more. With it, the Werebeasts who had come with her to the beach—excluding Ino and Izuna—took a step away.

—That moment. They vanished, leaving behind the high-frequency crack of splitting air.

* * *

""Eeeeeeeeeeeeeeeek!""

And a low-pressure field imploded with the rebound of the air punched out wholesale. It stirred up a little cyclone, forcing the remaining Werebeast girls to cling to a tree as they rode out the wind—but all who might have witnessed this sight…were gone.

⏻ CHAPTER 3
CHARMER
THE EMPRESS

—Oceand…the ocean-floor metropolis where Siren and Dhampir lived in symbiosis. An insular nation built on local production for local consumption, with almost no trade with other countries. Since it was at the bottom of the sea, it was impossible to visit by any sensible means. However, here was a group who had come by *means that were not sensible.* Jibril's shift after parting the sea had brought them to a vista overlooking all of Oceand. At a depth of about two hundred meters, when the seawater was displaced and then replaced—

"Well, that's how it goes, eh…"

The Shrine Maiden, groaning behind Sora, turned beyond the air membrane created by Jibril. There, the gravel and stones of the ocean floor swirled as if in a blender, raging madly…but however violent Jibril's magic might have been, the Covenants disallowed her from exercising force of arms. If she was able to execute it, it meant that it did not imply harm to anyone else, supposedly…

"Are you certain this isn't directly attacking the city or hitting anyone?"

"Y-yeah, the Ten Covenants are absolute. It's fine. I think. Probably."

Sora—thus reassured as the tide calmed and the gravel settled, the seawater clearing—said, "—Huhh, this is pretty cool."

"...Pretty..."

At the majesty of the city spread below, Sora and Shiro each shared their thoughts. In contrast to Sora's fairy-tale, pastoral image, it was actually a rather imposing metropolis. Countless structures stood in rows, apparently built of stacks of seafloor stone. The stone walls, glistening the color of pearl, were tiled with thin slices of coral and shells, creating a brilliant display of color. Perhaps utilizing the buoyancy of the water, there stood complex arches surely impossible to build on land, as well as buildings conspicuously shaped like inverted cones—and then Sora thought.

"...Hm? Why isn't everything blue?"

Only the blue light of the sun was supposed to penetrate to the ocean floor, but this question was answered by Shiro.

"...Brother, it must be...that."

What Shiro pointed to, floating through the sea, were countless fluorescent jellyfish and seaweed clumps—"streetlamps" utilizing natural bioluminescence.

—Oh, so the city illuminated itself.

"What the hell? Everyone keeps saying they're idiots, but this is a pretty nice city."

"...Ha-ha, thank youuu...," said Plum with a bitter smile full of resignation and self-deprecation. "We're the ones who built and manage it, you knowww...ah-ha-ha..."

...Unable to find words, Sora turned his gaze behind him. Jibril, Izuna, and Steph all looked around curiously, and the Shrine Maiden seemed wholly relaxed. And then there was—

"——King Sora, Sir... Just, what...is the meaning of this...?

Apparently having had his ears screwed up by the shift after all, Ino uttered his query through frequent fits of slight convulsing.

"Just like you asked, seems like *Izuna and the Shrine Maiden* are fine. You better tell Jibril thanks, you know?"

"...Ahh, that's right as rain, I suppose. But would you still allow me a word?"

Looking at Sora, Shiro, and Jibril one by one, the Shrine Maiden gave a deep, deep sigh. "—Could you lot use at least a little common sense..."

"Huh?"

"...What's, your...prob-lem?"

"Hmm, offshoot of the dog family of the cat order, wherein lies your objection?"

The trio who formed the perfect counterexample to common sense peered at her together. One of the few sensible members of the party, Steph, raised her voice in the Shrine Maiden's defense.

"*B-breaking through the sea* to approach—no matter how you look at it, it could scarcely appear more hostile!! Just how do you expect to be led to the queen at this rate!"

"We're the ones who were invited. They're the ones taking forever. We hurried to them in this urgent situation where their fate hangs by a thread. In consideration of Jibril's effort, they ought to greet us with a dance of appreciation and welcome, right?"

The Shrine Maiden and Izuna, who possessed the senses to detect Sora's *complete and utter bullshit*, frowned with half-open eyelids. The remaining Werebeast—Ino—was still writhing, covering his ears.

"...Ahh...I wouldn't worry about thaaat...look."

Even as Plum said this, everyone looking in the direction she was pointing saw countless shadows flying out of Oceand and heading their way in a big hurry.

—They had the tails of fish, covered in scales from the waist down, and the appearance of human women from the waist up. Other than having fins where their ears should have been, they didn't look that different from Immanities. The barest excuses for pieces of cloth covered their breasts, while their necks and arms were unduly ornamented. They appeared—indeed, just as in fairy tales—to be mermaids.

"...All right. So that's Siren. Great. Good thing it's like I pictured."

Sora, having been entirely ready to snap if the Deep Ones from the Cthulhu mythos showed up, was relieved, but then—

"L-look, everyone making such a flurry… We'll be reprimanded after all."

Steph whispered nervously as the Sirens swam right up to their membrane, and then—

"H-huh?"

Steph's eyes popped wide. The Sirens gyrated, undulating their bodies to and fro, showing off their brilliantly sparkling scales. Ornaments of coral and pearl flashed radiantly against their smooth, white skin. No consistent rhythm was detectable in the mermaids' movements. They gracefully interwove themselves through schools of multicolored fish, illuminated by the glowing jellyfish and the blue sunlight. The sight was fantastic enough to captivate everyone's attention—so it probably was exactly as he'd suggested.

"……Brother, this is their dance, of appreciation…and welcome."

"—Guess so… S-see, Steph, it's all cool, right?"

"What boundlessly tolerant creatures…"

Eventually, one Siren emerged, decorated in a manner gaudy even among such company. She beat her hands around and flapped her mouth for some reason. Steph looked on, puzzled, but Sora produced the answer immediately.

"We're in Jibril's air bubble; she's in the water—her voice must not be able to reach us."

"Indeeed…I'll go explain things and get some blood while I'm at iiit. I'll use that fuel to cast an underwater breathing spell on all of youuu, so after that, please dispel this wall of aiiir…"

With that, Plum set off at a trot, broke through the air membrane, and swam into the water. Watching her back:

"Even having said that we are the saviors come to rescue their race from destruction…"

"—Who would throw this sort of welcome after seeing such havoc wreaked right afore their city?"

Jibril and the Shrine Maiden whispered with gazes sharp, at which Sora smirked.

"…Siren, huh. Are they really that stupid, or—?"

"Hiii, guyyys, tee-hee-hee! ★ I'm Amila, the stand-in for the queeen. Mm, eeeverything's fiiine! ★"

They *were* stupid. Sora managed to swallow this frank opinion. The Siren who had come right away after Jibril dispelled the wall of air, this "Amila" chick, if you took her at her word—and, frighteningly enough, it did seem to be the truth—was, in fact, the effective agent plenipotentiary currently leading Siren. Beneath her rich, greenish hair slid sensual, fair skin. She had big, bright blue eyes. Coral jewelry adorned her entire body, but tastefully. This must have been the mermaids' formal dress. But what was inside—

"Thank you sooo muuuch for coming alll the way heeere! ★ Ohhhhh, goodness, there's no way I can express this feeling except to kiss you, righhht! Tee-hee-hee! Right?!"

"...Nah, let's just say it's the thought that counts..."

It wasn't even a question of formality at this point. Strictly speaking, she was speaking Immanity, but it was weird through and through. As Sora & Co. rolled their eyes, still Amila went on swimming pell-mell all around them

"Talk of you two has spread aaall the way down to the bottom of the ocean! The miracle king who saved Immanity, they said you were handsome, but now I see your face and you're just my type and you're so hot and *squeee*!! Right?! ★"

"Ahaah. I see."

It was the first time a girl had ever told him he was handsome, come to think of it...but strangely, Sora wasn't happy at all—.

"Aha! Your voice is sexy, too?! I'm sooooo wet! After all, we are in the oceaaan, tee-hee-hee!"

As he silently looked over to Plum, the Dhampir quietly returned his gaze, shaking her head sadly. With no sign of having noticed this, Amila went on with a bubbly smile.

"Ohh, yeahhh! We're preparing a party for you, tee-hee! ★ You want food? Or you want...*me?* ♥"

Foop—twisted the seductress Amila. Ready or not, behind Sora, Ino seemed to be heating up in more ways than one—

"Take me to your queen first. Save the hospitality for after we wake her up."

At Sora's curt dismissal, Ino somehow couldn't believe his ears.

But Amila said, not seeming to take it personally:

"Oh, you're so serious, juuust like they said! But you know what? Amila kinda admires that, aha!"

"...I see... Well, okay then, let's go."

"Surrre! Let's gooo! I'm gonna swim to the castle! Follow me, follow meee, tee-hee-heee! ♥"

Guided by Amila, Sora's party descended from the vista in the direction of Oceand.

Ino whispered into Sora's ear.

"...Sir, I am impressed at how promptly you managed to refuse."

"Unh?"

"Well, even we Werebeasts have our senses limited under the sea, so I cannot ascertain your inner thoughts, Sir...but to show no hesitation when faced with such an enticing lady, Sir. You have self-control that exceeds all imagination—"

His eyes half-lidded, Sora spat back at Ino.

"Gramps, are you out of your head? I may be a virgin, but what am I supposed to feel for that...? Let's go, Shiro."

"...Mm..."

Leaving Ino behind to gape, Sora grabbed Shiro and headed driftingly for the city—

■■■

Upon entering Oceand, they were greeted with ear-splitting cheers. Every Siren was bursting with smiles, dancing, seducing, playing off-tempo music. Their words—it perhaps not being necessary for them to speak Immanity—were a complete mystery, but their welcoming intent came through. Scattered here and there among these bustling Sirens could be seen some girls who appeared to be Dham-pirs. Their expressions, though, in contrast to the Sirens', tended to resemble Plum's. With miserable...smiles, their tired demeanors told Sora and his crew, *Thanks for coming all this way.*

—The Sirens provided a stable supply of blood, and the Dham-pirs helped the queen reproduce. This symbiotic relationship had worked perfectly well until the queen went to sleep and was now as a candle in the wind—and yet—

"Hey, why are these guys so cheerful when they're a step away from extinction?"

Indeed—the Dhampirs aside, the Sirens showed no sign of melan-choly whatsoever.

"...What, didn't I tell youuu...? They don't understaand it."

Jibril added to Plum's answer with a weary smirk.

"The foolishness of Siren reaches the status of legend. *Siren* has become a synonym for *fool* in the idioms of every race's language, and in fact, it is even used as a verb in some."

Sora's party walked the ocean floor as they followed Amila.

—Underwater ambulation. Confused as to whether it was swim-ming or walking, Shiro proceeded on Sora's arm. As for Ino, Izuna, and the Shrine Maiden—what would you expect of Werebeasts? They had already figured out how to move in these circumstances and were advancing with languorous, bouncing strides. Meanwhile, Jibril, despite being underwater, was still "flying."

"—Hey, so Immanity is supposed to be beneath this globally rec-ognized race of idiots?"

It was true that right now the ones most obviously struggling were Sora and Shiro, but still.

"Before I met you, my masters, I would have answered, 'Yes'—but perhaps this would be a better way to put it: They are ranked one above Immanity purely by virtue of having a special nature, but they are the race that represents the extreme of stupidity."

Plum followed the smirking Jibril with an ephemeral grin. "They

have no skills other than to eat, sleep, screw, and play, you seeee...
You know how fish contain things that make you smarter, but fish
themselves are stupid...? It's a mysteryyy."

This world really doesn't have any races that get along, does it? Sora
thought with distant eyes.

"...Well, when you consider that the de facto agent plenipotentiary is *her*..."

"Oh, no... Her Highness Amila is actually far and away one of the
best, if only by virtue of being able to speak the Immanity tongue..."

She was one of the best—. Sora glanced at Plum compassion-
ately. Plum accepted his look with one of infinite, long-suffering
forbearance.

"Well, we're in the same boat, as they sayyy... The plan and methodology for you to help us—as well as the idea of intervening in the
queen's dreams itself—were all concocted by uuus...They don't even
have the concept of work. About the only thing they're good at is
matiiing, ha-ha...ha..."

".......Must be rough, kid..."

Guided by Amila, they entered a building that was tall even by
Oceand standards. While being guided, suddenly Sora mentioned
something that had crossed his mind.

"Speaking of mating, Jibril... Sirens have kids with men of other
races, right?"

"Yes, that is so."

"Are there any 'half-breed' Ixseeds crossing races?"

—It hadn't been long since Sora and Shiro had come to this world,
but, in fantasy worlds, there were often "half-elves" and stuff—but
he didn't remember hearing of any such "half-breeds" here. That
was as it should be, Jibril declared.

"*There are not.* The Ixseeds do have some similarities in appearance, but their souls are completely dissimilar."

—There was that "soul" again. This entity that had not been demonstrated in Sora and Shiro's old world apparently was common
sense in this one. It must be like chromosomes, Sora decided on his

own as he continued. "But Sirens mate with other races, right? So doesn't that make half-Sirens?"

"No, what is born is strictly a Siren."

"Even though you're using two souls?"

"Just as Dhampirs obtain soul from blood, Sirens obtain soul from *mating* and transform it to create copies of themselves. It is because this is less efficient than the reproduction of ordinary living things that the partner is sucked dry."

"...Still pretty sick."

"I wonder? Strictly speaking with reference to literature—it is said to be a pleasure that ascends to the heavens."

"You mean the 'ascend' part literally, don't you...and it's a one-way trip."

But, all right—in any case—

"This is why half-breeds—children inheriting the traits of different races—cannot be born."

Hmm...Sora pondered. *I guess it's because they're indivisible that Tet designated them as "sixteen seeds."*

"—Jibril, is there something on my face?"

Sora noticed Jibril staring at him.

"I believe I mentioned that Flügel are not 'living things.'"

"Yeah...you said they're 'living beings' or something."

"Therefore, our *souls are amorphous*. It would theoretically be possible to intake a bit of soul through copulation and synthesize it with my own to form a child into definite shape. It would only be virtual, mind you, but in a sense, it would be possible to have the child of an individual of another race."

"—I'm not really seeing what you're getting at."

Lowering her head reverently, moving her halo to the back of her head, folding her wings—a posture of loyalty shown only to her lord—Jibril clasped her hands together as if in prayer and spoke.

"All you must say is '*Bear my child,*' and your humble servant, Jibril, will be ready at any time to become great with—"

*   *   *

"...Jibril...STF, U..."

Jibril found herself forcibly silenced by one sharp word from Shiro, but their guide was oblivious.

"Weeeeeee're! Heeeeere!"

Sora raised his head at the high-pitched voice that subsequently rang out.

"Here we arrre! This is the chamber of the queeeen!"

Amila put her hand on the door, slowly pushed it open—

—and light spilled out.

The chamber of the queen was quite expansive and draped with a pink ceiling curtain and carpet. On the walls, seaweed emitting soft light was woven into regular patterns to illuminate the room. Stained glass canopied the high ceiling, which allowed what sunlight reached as far as the ocean floor into the room. But even this faint light seemed unnecessary due to the giant crystal on the throne below that emanated a presence that was almost blinding—. No, it only was beautiful and clear enough to look like a crystal...it was actually a mass of ice.

"___......"

All who laid eyes on it were lost for words. Solemnly—or at least doing her best to attempt solmenity—Amila announced:

"May I introduce—the queen of Siren...Her Majesty...Queen Laila Lorelei."

—Inside the ice, a beauty slept. Blue hair, rolling like the sea, draped over her young, almost translucent face. Her white limbs, decorated in dazzling gold, faded to seductive scales from the thighs. Reflecting the light that illuminated the room, they seemed to sparkle with a rainbow. The queen, wrapped in light and gold inside a coffin of ice, had her eyes quietly closed on the open-shell throne. At the back of the speechless party, Plum spoke with Amila.

"Oh, Your Highness Amila... It's about waking Her Majesty, buuut...King Sora and the others heeere...say they want to all try the game *togetherrr*... Is that okaaay?"

At Plum's words, Amila briefly made a face but repled:

"Whaaat? I don't miiind! Is it okay with youuu?"

"Yeeess...S-sooo, I'd like about thirty assistants to help compile the riiite."

Amila nodding, *mmm-hmmm.* "Okay! Then I'll go do the things to wake up the queen, all righhht! Since you're all going to do magic, you'll need blood, too, won't youuu, tee-hee-hee! Amila's going to go get some more girls for you, so please do your best, Pluuum!"

"Righhht... O-okay, then, I'll be off to get the rite ready to enter the queen's dreaaams..."

With a bow, Amila and Plum made their exits from the room.

Seemingly oblivious to this exchange, the rest of the party stood staring at the ice in which the queen slept.

"Wh-what a comely lady..."

Steph went off heatedly as if she'd forgotten they were the same gender. In fact, the queen's alluring figure made not only Ino, but even Jibril, the Shrine Maiden, and Izuna all gawk, entranced—but—

"Hmmg...? You think she's all that pretty, Shiro?"

"...I...dun-no..."

"Whaaaaaat—?!"

As Sora and Shiro muttered quizzically together, everyone else gaped at them.

"A-are you two out of your minds?! Wh-what would you call her if not beautiful?!"

"...Hey, you're the one who needs to chill. I'm just saying she's nothing to get all worked up about."

Sora groused and knitted his brow, annoyed by Steph's outburst. He looked at the queen again.

—Laila Lorelei, the mermaid princess sleeping in a coffin of ice. Her appearance was, sure, pretty nice. But, Sora could clearly assert—she wasn't all that. It wasn't like, for example, Jibril's violent beauty capable of silencing works of art. Nor did it resemble the divinely bewitching attractiveness the Shrine Maiden had displayed under the moonlight. It didn't have Izuna's innocent cuteness, not to speak of—

"...? Brother...?"

Addressing the searching expression of his sister beside him, Sora declared, "Yeah. —*Not even worth comparing.* I mean, even Steph's better-looking than that."

"...! Y-you can't appease me with such transparent flattery?!"

"No, what would be the point of me trying to flatter you now..."

Behind the incredulous Sora, Ino quietly patted his shoulders.

"King Sora......... Ah, never mind. It's quite all right."

And he continued in a gentle tone.

"There is no cause for concern—impotency can be cured. I recommend softshell turtle stew—"

"That is not how it is! Don't slander me!"

Shouting and jabbing a finger at the ice as if to say, *I mean,* Sora howled:

"Stop and think about it!! I'm not saying she's ugly, but is she anything to get worked up over when we've got the Shrine Maiden, Jibril, Izuna, and Shiro? Our beauties are all literally off the charts!"

Steph and Ino still glared as if looking at something sad—but at Sora's words, Jibril and the Shrine Maiden alone came around.

"I-indeed my master is wise... That is the *special characteristic* of Siren I mentioned earlier."

"—Huh?"

The Shrine Maiden and Jibril averted their eyes from the ice, and Jibril continued.

"Sirens, though lacking the traits of physical excellence and magic, are able to survive principally thanks to their one weapon, on display here...namely—" She took a breath. "As long as they are in the sea—they can attract anything.

"Siren is a race beloved of the sea—the reason that they *live in the sea and cannot leave the sea* is that, in their bodies, they possess a plethora of spirits...water spirits capable of attracting any other spirits."

"...Oh..."

"Oh, it's like that."

That makes sense, nodded Sora and Shiro, as it finally came together. How Siren, who, before the Ten Covenants, reproduced by devouring the men of other races, was able to survive without leaving the ocean and without possessing outstanding powers or magic. In other words—they just had to *charm* potential threats. That explained how they were able to swim with the schools of fish and how they were able to withstand the water pressure of the deep sea without magic.

"And this charm we're talking about isn't a magical charm?"

"It is not. It is simply a matter of the flow of spirits—a sort of *magnetism* that works on spirits. It is simply a feature of the race... Under normal circumstances, this would be no matter for concern, but—"

Glancing at the queen and looking away again.

"This fish-woman—seems to have a quantity of spirits that is truly exceptional."

Jibril muttered, apparently unnerved by the fact that she could not escape the queen's effects. Likewise, even having known that— the Shrine Maiden scratched her head with a look of weariness. But then—

Hmm, murmured Jibril. "On the other hand...why does it not affect you, my masters?"

"...Mmm...? Jibril, you said, we...don't, have, spirits."

"Yeah, you said all living things in this world have spirits in their bodies, but Shiro and I don't."

When they first met, they'd let Jibril check Sora's body for spirits as proof that they were from another world. If it was a magnetism that worked on spirits, it should have come as no surprise that it didn't work on Sora or Shiro—but.

"No, if you have a soul, you undoubtedly have spirits. They must simply be unknown to me or somehow evade my detection. But then why would you be unaffected? Let's see..."

Jibril mumbled on, the object of her interest seemingly having shifted back to Sora and Shiro, as she surveyed them with sparkling eyes.

—Meanwhile, Ino suggested offhandedly, "Could it not be more simply explained in terms of King Sora's virility?"

"You shut up, old fart. You're just a dick-thinking horndog, whereas I am a model of reason."

"Thaaanks for waitiiiiiiiing!"

—Amila and Plum burst back into the chamber. They seemed to have finished preparing the rite to enter the queen's dreams or whatever. This having been accomplished—the two approached the ice in which the queen slept.

"'Kay, now we're gonna use the spell Plum and everyone made to take you into the queen's dreaaams." Her disarming smile unchanged, Amila continued casually.

"Everyone who's going to wake up the queeen, *wager everything* by the Covenants and then touch the crystal, okayyy?"

——……

"What? Um, what are you saying?"

The one who broke the silence was Steph, but Amila replied vacantly. "Huh, is there a problem?"

"Of course there's a problem. What are you saying?!"

…Wager everything? In other words, bet all your property, status, rights, and life—literally everything?

"Why do we need to do that?! I thought you were the ones who *asked* us to come save you?!"

"Whaaaa…? Plum, didn't you explain it to them before you caaame?"

"Nghh…I-I'm sorry…"

Plum desperately apologized to Amila as she put a finger to her dismayed face. But they were interrupted—

"Cool it, Steph. The one who's confused is *you*."

—Sora interceded calmly and plainly. At his improbable composure, Steph turned back and looked around at everyone. Sora and Shiro—the Shrine Maiden and Jibril—even Ino and Izuna—all looked as if the situation was obvious.

"They called us here—to beat *the queen's game* and wake her up.

"Third of the Ten Covenants: Play for wagers that each agrees are of equal value. The queen set up the game when she went to sleep, by the Covenants, saying 'make me fall in love with you if you dare,' so if we wanna win the queen's love, we have to put our money on the table—right?"

"Yeah, yeah, that's a hottie for you! Not only is your face handsome, your brain's handsome, too!"

Amila nodded with a girly laugh—but the Shrine Maiden and Shiro smiled, subtly, thinly, and Sora was the only one who noticed. But Steph, completely missing this subtle exchange, continued as if unconvinced.

"That-that's absurd," she insisted. Her voice swelling even more shrilly, she went on. "They're the ones who are in trouble! Why should we bear such risk when we came to save them?!"

But Sora still took it in stride.

"Plum said meddling in someone's feelings and dreams would normally be disallowed by the Ten Covenants, but we can do it 'cos the queen allows us—but her consent only goes as far as the *game*."

—i.e.

"If we don't start the queen's game first, we can't use our spells, and, of course, we can't wake her up. So the ante the queen's demanding for us to play her—"

Looking at Plum and Amila, Sora clowned.

"It's like, 'If you want my love, you'd better be ready to give up everything!' …Right?"

Steph was stunned into silence, and the faces of the rest each assumed their own shocked expressions. Amila alone tore into Sora with a surfeit of praise.

"Thaaaat's righhht! Ohh, can't *I* have you instead of the queeen!"

Sora ignored the boisterous Amila. "Well, we've got a spell that will make the queen fall in love for sure, so I guess it's fine."

"Y-yeeess! I guarantee iiit; leave it to meee!"

"B-but that's—I mean, what if for some reason the spell doesn't work?!" Steph was still unable to shake off her unease.

"Then you can just leave it to Amilaaa," Amila decisively declared.

"Even though the queen can play the game, she'll still be asleep if she wins, and Amila's the one in charge of her stuff! Even if something goes wrong, I'll just give it all back to you, so there's no risk!"

"Wait, we can't count on—"

But Sora cut her off.

"Sure, no problem, then. So, shall we begin the game?"

—This is weird, Steph thought to herself. Something about this was definitely off. In the first place, why would such a high-risk condition only be brought up at this point? Why do they think nothing of it, Steph wondered, looking at Sora. It wasn't like him. To go along with such a fishy game—. But Steph looked around again. Seeing that no one else seemed to think anything at all of it, she closed her lips tightly. *Wh-what is this...? What is going on!*

Now, then, began Plum as she started explaining the rules.

"Everyone, please swear by the Covenants that you wager everything and touch the iiice. Then I'll cooperate with everyone downstairs to deploy the rite and magically lead you into the queen's dreaams...then I'll be coming along to help you with the 'cheat,' okayyy...?"

As Plum steadily wove together the rite, she elaborated:

"Since it's a dream, the situation can be anything you waant... Your representative—it's King Sora, righhht? King Sora's imagination will form the foundation to build the situation in the queen's dreaam... Regardless of the situation—there is only one victory conditiooon."

Continuing on Plum's theme, Sora took over.

"If someone makes the queen fall in love and wake up, they win, and if they get rejected, they lose—and the losers are out of the game and have to pay up everything they bet. That's what we're swearing by the Covenants, right?"

"Y-yeeess… B-but."

But. I know, Sora interrupted.

"We've got Plum's cheat, and even if we lose, we can get it all back from Amila—right? Relax."

Sora delivered this with a bold—yet to Steph, somehow off—grin.

"With this crew, under these conditions, there's not a chance in a million we'll lose, so let's get this on."

"O-okayyy. Then, King Sora, please imagine a situatioon, and—"

At her words, Sora imagined the single game you had to think of when it came to the romance genre.

"Please make your declaratiooon!"

"—Aschente!"

Sora, Shiro, Steph, Jibril, the Shrine Maiden, Ino, Izuna, and Plum. Together, the instant they said it, found their consciousnesses going white.

—Soon the white was repainted in blue. As if waking from a dream, their cloudy collective consciousness floated up. Blood flowed through all the slack parts of their bodies, and feeling returned—and then.

"Urbrbrbrbubrbugabrb?"

…They were drowning. In the middle of the great blue sea, Sora and Shiro, Izuna, Ino, and even the Shrine Maiden were being overwhelmed by the waves. The burning taste of brine. Pain stabbed through and past their nostrils. Calm thinking went out the window—yet, in their brains, a different vision played.

—As there are beginnings, so there will be endings…

Sparkling, gaudy visuals. With sound effects like spewing stardust, the monotone of a narrator somewhere coolly continued.

As there are meetings, so shall there be part—

"Is this the time to be chilling with the opening movie?!"

Desperately thrusting his face out of the surface of the sea, Sora raised a cry.

"In what world has *Tok*meki* ever started with you drowning? 'Heartbeat,' my ass!"

Well, it was true that his pulse was significantly raised. But he would have preferred not to describe the palpitations of imminent death as "Heartbeat Memorial."

"Oh, s-sorryyy... Your image and the queen's got a little mixed up, and it's taking some time to build the environmeent... Hold on just a biiit—"

If you thought about it, it wasn't surprising. Even if they were able to meddle in the queen's dreams, it wasn't as if the kind of school stories that existed in Sora and Shiro's world would exist in this world. It was only natural that work would have to be done to make Sora's image compatible with the queen's frame of reference—but—

"...Brother...it was, a good...life..."

"Pluuum! My sister's already giving up on life! Get it dooone!"

Shiro closed her eyes with a beatific smile in his arms as Sora screamed.

"—Uh, uh, rite build complete, configuring setting, now applying changeees!"

—That instant. The setting in which they had been drowning in the sea was overwritten as if turning the page of a book. From the surface of the sea to the ocean floor—the scene shifted. The unwanted parameter of breathing was gone. As if turning over cards one by one, the changes optimal in the dream world for the administration of the game were gradually added, and things became more convenient.

"—Master, are you all right?!"

At Jibril's strong voice, Sora came to. Before he knew it, ground had been put under his feet.

"…Y-yeah… Damn, that was close…"

In the transparent blue sea, Sora let out a "deep breath" and wiped the "sweat from his brow." Holding close Shiro, who was quivering from the fear of almost drowning, he muttered as if groaning.

"If you get off on weird scenarios like endings where you die right after the game begins, I'd really rather you do it somewhere else."

"…I knew it, going to the beach…sucks…"

"This sea which has placed my masters in mortal peril—I suppose it must be eliminated outright."

"Why can't you just learn to swim…?"

Steph, apparently the only one who had been fine so far, chimed in with half-closed eyes. Beside her, though, the Shrine Maiden and the other Werebeasts irritatedly agreed with Jibril.

"…Right you are. What's this ocean for? Who created this big, outlandish puddle?"

"For once, I must agree with Miss Jibril. We would all be better off if the sea were dry and gone."

"And the sea stinks, please… It should just go away and leave us the fish, please."

Now fully immersed in the dream, each took their turn at revilement as they gradually regained their composure.

—Sora, Shiro, Steph, Jibril, the Shrine Maiden, Ino, and Izuna. Each now having his or her feet squarely on the ground, they watched as the setting was constructed before them. Despite being at the bottom of the ocean, the blue sky shone overhead, and clouds floated across the shimmering surface of the sea. The undulating terrain was flattened, and, on the ocean floor previously littered only with rock and coral, a school appeared. The tropical fish that wandered around them were transformed into nameless NPCs. In just about the time it took to blink, the fictional setting of an ocean-floor school was created before their eyes.

A high school built in Oceand's architectural style… As Sora regarded this bizarre scene, a voice piped up beside him:

"I'm most surprised that Her Majesty knew what a school was at alll... She must have read it in a book, I suppose," conjectured Plum, apparently having likewise finished diving into the dream. She grasped the meaning of Sora's gaze and announced with a tired smile tinged with bitterness, "Ha-ha... There's no such thing as a school in Oceeeand... What would they studyyy?"

The scenery having finished changing, now Sora and crew found themselves being gradually modified. First—in their vision, countless icons lit up.

"...? What is this?"

As Steph tried to touch these oddities in her vision but found her hand sweeping through empty space, Sora explained.

"It's the user interface...the command menu."

—It was just like the status bar in a romance simulation game. Considering the scene that recalled *Tok*Meki*, just as he'd imagined, Sora continued.

"...If you're capable of recreating this, I wish you wouldn't drop us in the sea."

"Well, it's only recreated for the playerrs... To build the setting, it took a little more work to get your image and the queen's memories working togetherrr... And now that you mention it." Plum asked, suddenly suspicious, "Sir, *where did you pick up* that image? I've never seen the likes of iiit..."

Not knowing that Sora and Shiro were *from another world*, Plum was bothered by the source of their information—but was ignored.

"So, things that only affect the players are easier to change, huh?"

"Uh, yeeess, and I'm still building the riiite...so if you would please continue imaginiiing.

"However," Plum added as she went on, "you cannot change your appearance, age, or seeex...so please take nooote..."

—The queen slept, hoping for the appearance of a prince. If she was to wake up and see the one she had fallen in love with, only to find that his profile pic was totally fake—she'd probably go back to sleep. That was fine. The real issue was—

"If we can change our *names*, make mine Kon*mi Man."

"...Brother, starting...with all stats at 573, is cheating..."

At his sister's chiding through half-closed eyes, Sora grinned boldly and shook his finger, *tsk, tsk.*

"Easter eggs are part of the game. Plus, with that trick, as soon as you try to do something, you get sick and end up taking the whole first year off and missing all the events... See, there are disadvantages, too, right?"

"...Okay, then, I'm...gonna be, Sem*ponume..."

"...Excuse me, what do those meaaan...?"

As they jabbered—now the players' outfits changed to match Sora's image. Sora was just wearing a blazer over his usual "I ♥ PPL" shirt.

"...Hmm, this clothing is a bit constricting."

Likewise dressed in a boy's school uniform—the ninety-eight-year-old sinewed geezer complained next to him.

"...A uniform stretched out by bulging muscles...I think I'm gonna have nightmares."

With this grumble, Sora turned his gaze from hell to heaven—in other words, to the ladies. Shiro, beside him, was dressed not in her usual all black—but a brightly colored girls' uniform.

—Mixing Sora's image with the queen's, it was a sailor suit a bit on the revealing side. And, surrounding her, in the same sailor suits, were Izuna, Jibril, and the Shrine Maiden—

"...The Shrine Maiden in a sailor suit. Gotta say that's awesome, but..."

"What, have you a complaint?"

Sweeping up her long, golden hair, the Shrine Maiden spoke, clad in the same brilliant sailor suit as Shiro. Her two tails swaying, the legs that peeked out from under her lifted skirt were nothing short of dazzling—but.

"...Hey, Shrine Maiden, come to think of it, how old are you?"

"Did no one teach you it's rude to ask a lady her age?"

"I guess... By the way, you're the one who created the Eastern Union, right?"

Flinch. The Shrine Maiden reacted.

"You even said yourself it was from as far back as you can remember. Izuna's eight, and she remembers things. The Eastern Union's meteoric rise over half a century—even if we don't take into account the time it took to establish the Eastern Union, that makes you at least fifty-eight—"

"Let me teach you something interesting, you hairless monkey. Werebeasts—especially bloodbreak individuals—age slowly."

Interrupting Sora's on-the-mark reasoning, the Shrine Maiden spoke with a dazzling smile.

—That suddenly turned dangerous, and in an entrancing voice, she warned:

"If you try calling me 'old lady'—you know what'll happen. ♥"

"—Hf... Shrine Maiden, let me tell you something interesting, too."

But Sora took it head-on and countered.

"*Looks are everything!* You give the feeling of being older from your behavior and tone, but, looks-wise, you're a hot twenty-year-old at worst—in which case, your actual age is of no consequence. This is one of the basic precepts of Immanity."

"...It's *your* precept."

Blatantly ignoring Steph's contribution to the conversation, Sora pointed to the side.

"Anyway, we've got an over-sixty here, too, so it's nothing to worry about."

"Oh, Master, to be precise, I am 6,407 years of age."

Having examined her own clothes with curiosity, Jibril answered with a smile. In Jibril's case, the wings at her hips pulled up at her top, flashing her belly button, which was also *subsequent description omitted.* Meanwhile—

"...By the way, may I ask one question?"

"Mm—what is it, Steph?"

"Why am I the only one dressed like you and Mr. Ino—in the *boys' uniform*?"

—Yes. Shiro, Jibril, the Shrine Maiden, and Izuna were all wearing the girls' sailor suit, but Steph alone wore the same blazer as Sora and Ino. Nodding deeply, Sora revealed the mystery.

"Good question—there's a saying, 'To shoot the general, first shoot his horse.'"

"...What?"

All eyes were suddenly focused on Sora, who explained with a serious mien:

"—First, why I didn't dress everyone up like guys: two reasons."

He raised a finger, ticking off his reasoning—

"One, if you're going for the main heroine, you wanna get her friends—so having *girls helping you* is important."

"...You sure know how to talk like a cad with a fine placid expression..."

The Shrine Maiden spoke for everyone rolling their eyes as she offered this feedback. Paying her no mind, though, and raising a second finger, Sora continued.

"And two—you gotta consider the potential trap that the queen isn't interested in guys in the first place."

"...Didn't I say that the queen is looking for a man with the ability to reproduuuce?"

"You presented no compelling evidence."

To Plum, looking cynical as well, Sora declared this decisively and went on.

"Now, as for the reason I put Steph in drag—Steph has high social skills and will make a fine informant."

Had it been a matter strictly of political ability, the Shrine Maiden could also have been a candidate—but. Sora's intuition told him that Steph would be better in terms of personal relationships.

"I wanted a guy friend who was as in the know as *Yoshio*, with the friending chops, too—but..."

Sora turned back to Steph and heaved a deep sigh.

"...If I gotta compare...you're more like *Ijuuin*..."

"—What? I don't really follow..."

—Indeed, with red hair and balanced features, a dashing young man appearing to be of a higher social class— (The cross-dressing Steph was utterly puzzled.) Free of sarcasm, seemingly unaware of his appearance but accomplished in both physical and literary feats, while even appearing to have a domestic side. Skilled in conversation, bold in practical action, and even—strong willed, his gaze clear. Still, behind it all, showing a glimpse of deep kindness, even forbearance—such a fine young man.

—Frankly speaking, Sora had the impulse to punch such an enemy of the unreal world—a good-looking guy with a life—and again he sighed.

"...Ijuuin? Who is that?"

"...From the first game...don't, worry about it..."

"...Come to think of it, wouldn't it be faster just to seduce her with Steph instead of Gramps?"

"Huh? Wait, I can't seduce a lady—and, I mean...So-Sora—"

"...Ah, it seems the rite has been fully buiiilt!"

■■■

"Ahem, now let us play the opening once more—and then we will bring in the queen's consciousness as wellll."

Simultaneous to Plum's pronouncement, a giant screen was projected before them. The crappy trailer that earlier had been injected into their brains played along to a bouncy soundtrack. After showing pinups of the school and classrooms along with narration, the scene moved to the courtyard, where a giant crimson coral formation extended countless branches radially, the camera capturing it at a slightly upward angle. The narrator explained calmly:

* * *

Kagayaki Marine High School... It is said that those who confess their love under its legendary coral find true love—

At the familiar phrasing, Sora groaned, his eyelids at half-mast.

"...Hey. A legendary tree is one thing, but 'legendary coral,' what the hell is that...?"

Confessing under an old tree made sense. The sound of bells and a hill swept with flittering cherry blossoms, okay. But under the "legendary coral"? Are you freaking kidding?

"I don't know what to sayyy... There aren't any trees in the ocean, you seeee..."

—*And, actually, coral's pretty gross when you look at it closely, right?* Sora thought, but, regardless of his opinion on the matter, the opening continued.

—After a while, the boring narration ended, and now pop music played. Against a pink background, under the "legendary coral," there could be seen a mermaid with long, billowing blue hair.

—The queen. The sailor-suited queen—Laila—swam under the giant red coral formation as if quietly dancing. The brilliant uniform enwreathing her supple limbs flapped in the brine, further eliciting the queen's seductive charms, as even the scaled tail that extended from her short skirt gave off an impression of luster as it moved the water. The queen, her gaze somehow melancholic, stretched her hands toward the sky as if longing for something, and—

"La—— ♪"

Sang.

—All who heard her voice drew a collective breath.

"Gracious...!"

"Hmm, this is something... A beauty is a beauty even in her voice."

Steph and Ino voiced their astonishment. The queen who could entrance most anyone who merely saw her visage—. Her singing voice possessed a beauty to make the souls of listeners tingle with narcotic pleasure.

...All except for Sora and Shiro. The two watched the screen with disinterested demeanors. "I'm starting to get the feeling we just have weird tastes..."

Her voice aside, the pop song and the video did not remotely complement the queen's sensual poses and wistful expression. Well, in the first place, she was entirely too sexy not to look ridiculous in a sailor suit. It was like one of those "thirty-something" women (ha) trying to cosplay as a high school girl—

"Well, to each his own, I guess...but you're telling us to conquer that?"

Just can't get the motivation... Sora subtly sighed.

■ DAY 1 ■

—Suddenly, a field displaying "Day 1" appeared in everyone's vision. It was a familiar sight to Sora and Shiro, but Plum explained for the sake of the rest.

"Umm, I think you should see several 'commands' displayed. These can be used to select from a certain range of actiooons... For instance, you can give giiifts."

At Plum's words, Sora tilted his head. "I thought you said this was a real-life romance game? And there are no hidden parameters like Affection...?"

"...Brother." Shiro held something out to the mumbling Sora. "...'Gift'...command... Brother, did your, Affection, go up?" Shiro asked with anticipatory eyes, but Sora responded with a wry smile.

"Sorry, Sister. My affection for you is already maxed out; it's too late—"

"Then, Master, if I may be so bold—"

Jibril jumped in. Averting her eyes from this exchange, Plum continued her explanation.

"Um... Among the commands displayed, you should see two heart icooons."

They all checked and found them immediately. Lower left-hand side of the command panel. There was an ordinary heart symbol, and then there was another with a plus sign added.

"These hearts represent the 'Confess' commaaand… It is up to you how to confess your love, but, if you select this and are rejected, it will be considered a loooss… And the one with a plus sign—"

"Is your 'love spell'—the cheat command, right? Okay, I get the setup…so."

Sora, having quickly grasped the game system, turned to Ino.

"Okay, Gramps, if you've wedded thirty brides, you've got to have banged a few more, right? Go show us your accursed technique that would put Taka Kat*u to shame and, whoosh, snap up that queen for us."

"The manner of your wording irks me to no end, Sir, but…"

"I'm looking forward to seeing these romancing techniques you pride yourself on, Ino Hatsuse," said the Shrine Maiden to the sour-faced Ino.

"…Grampy, go for it, please."

"Understood! If the Holy Shrine Maiden commands…!"

Ino responded deferentially to the two voices of encouragement offered, and he turned again to Sora.

"…Sir, I have till now been listening in silence, but your talk of shooting the horse to shoot the general and of collaborators and informants escapes my understanding entirely."

"…Say whaaat?"

Ino raised his hands and continued despite Sora's furrowed brow.

"…Sir, surely you are not considering ignoring the tastes and preferences of a lady and imposing one's own inclinations—not to speak of feigning the personality the lady seeks—as *love*?"

…Frankly, yeah, he was. "Well, that's what I consider a love *sim*, at the very least."

Ino directed a serious grimace at the choked-for-words Sora. "Hff…I see. In that case, it was indeed wise to entrust this to me. Just as mastering fighting games does not make one a master fighter, mastering romance games does not make one capable of real-life romance."

—That was quite right, but somehow the fact that his confidence was based on a mountain of actual sexual achievement was irritating.

"Sir, I wonder if you see why it is you are a virgin—an unpopular, socially incompetent, hopelessly pathetic young man?"

"...Old fart, I'm gonna have Jibril warp you beyond the stars."

Sora looked at him with a stormy gaze, but Ino paid no mind.

"There are those who say that romance is a mind game—*but then why do you not succeed, Sir?*"

".........Mnrg?"

—If it was a mind game, Sora ought to have been able to play it far better than Ino. At Ino's well-reasoned, all-out implicit defense of Sora's intrinsic ability, Sora swallowed his words.

"I see. Love takes on a different form for each individual. However...ultimately, it comes down to conveying one's feelings."

Ino fixed keen eyes upon Sora.

—What lay in those eyes, though, was not the color of disdain. Nor irony, nor hatred, nor pity, nor spite. With eyes that—Sora knew them well, eyes that *he had seen directed at him more than he'd cared to admit in his old world*—Ino spoke.

"The words of a charlatan such as yourself, who lives atop a stack of lies, cannot possibly accomplish such a thing."

Yes, they were—eyes of distrust.

"However, there is one thing to be said. It may be a mind game in just one respect—specifically—"

With these words, Ino looked at his controls and continued.

"—The first one there wins."

Unhesitatingly selecting the "Confess" heart—Ino ran off.

""Wha—?!""

Leaving the stupefaction of Sora & Co. behind—with raging speed that did justice to the physical prowess of Werebeast—Ino charged. The gaze of the dashing Ino, with steps resounded like explosions, fixed on just one thing: the queen on the verge of entering through the school gate—Laila. Toward her back as she walked with an entourage of several NPCs, Ino bellowed:

"Oh, beautiful young miss! Please pause to hear my tale!"

At the great voice that evoked thoughts of a knight on a battlefield announcing his name and particulars, the queen slowly turned. The aquamarine of her eyes took in Ino—and she responded.

"Are you calling me...?"

—Even these few words were like notes of a melody from heaven.

"......! Of course!"

For a moment, Ino forgot the game. Each little word and movement of the beauty before him rushed inward to melt his soul. But, shaking his head, *no, no,* Ino put strength into his belly.

—He could fall for her. In fact, he'd *have* to fall for her. He gritted his teeth and steeled up his eyes.

—But he couldn't be sucked in. He must be the one to swallow her...!

"Fair maiden, forgive me for interrupting you so suddenly. If you have a heart—I would have you hear my words."

"My—what's the matter?"

The queen flashed a soft smile. It was enough to make Ino feel as if his heart had been grasped and squeezed. He wanted to grab and throw away everything—such was the temptation. The queen's gaze, the queen's voice, the queen's expression, her fair nape. The angle of her fingers nonchalantly put to her chest, the shadow cast by her silkily swaying hair— These things could not be perceived but as an ineffable crown jewel...!

—*Could it be?* Ino wondered. That the challengers of the past had been sucked in by the queen's pulchritude to the point of being unable to express their love? Such beauty. Such violent splendor. Indeed, before such a woman, none of the youngbloods here or there could conceivably say a word. But Ino...returned a soft smile.

—Not a comfortable smile. Comfort was out of the question. Love was not a mind game—no, it was a *battle*. The act of smiling was first and foremost a kind of attack—rooted in instinct not unlike a beast baring his fangs.

Slowly, heavily, Ino went to his knees.

—*Love.* He thrust his palms to the heavens as if praying and then smacked them forcefully upon the earth.

—*Love was*— He glared at the woman powerfully with both eyes—not a threat. It was a silent declaration of war.

—*A thing to be won.* To be taken with one's own hands. He pressed his palms to the ground, neatly aligned with his knees, and bowed his forehead, his skull with it, deep down…!

—It left no room for argument. A fine, formal—

"Please! I beg you! Would you please make hot, passionate love with me for a single nighhht——!"

—genuflection.

——……

""————Whaat?""

—Whose voices were these? Perhaps everyone's. To say nothing of Sora and crew, the queen gaped, dumbfounded, while Ino heedlessly forged ahead.

"Since the moment I first laid eyes on you, my heart has boiled like magma. Behold! My pride and joy has risen to the firmness of steel—!!"

"Eegh…"

The queen held her breath, lost her smile, and backed away. But Ino raised his voice still louder and pressed on…!

"Please, please forgive me, queen of the sea! But it is your beauty that is at fault! The very instant I spied you, I have been helpless before this surging impulse to hold and penetrate you! Can you not find it in your heart to grasp the feelings that burn within me!"

"He's—he's genuflecting so hard she doesn't even have time to cringe?!"

Sora shivered. Could this, of all things, be the perfect strategy

of the man who had taken thirty wives?! As the entire assemblage withered to absolute zero, Ino's passionate genuflection proceeded unabated.

"I beg you! I beg you! Let us make love! Let us make hot, passionate love!"

"Uh, wait, no, I...um..."

The queen had heard any number of declarations of love from those who had disturbed her dreams since she had consigned herself to slumber. Despite having brushed off every common sort of man, this must have been her first encounter with such a direct approach, for she panicked and scrambled to flee into the school. And yet—!

"Please wait!"

Grshh— Ino's sinewed hand seized the queen's arm and restrained her.

"No, hey, let me go—!"

"I shall not! I shall never let you go! I would that you apprehend the pounding in my chest, the fire in my loins! Though I be but a shriveled old bag of bones, I shall stake my life to ensure that you know true satisfaction!!"

"Noooooooooooooo!!"

——No words. This was verging on criminal—no, actually, this was some straight-up sick shit unfolding right before their eyes. If there were a temperature below absolute zero, that would describe the atmosphere among Sora and his fellow spectators.

"......Hey, but."

Sora, keeping his distance as he watched, fearfully asked the Shrine Maiden...

"You were saying the old man's snagged thirty wives with that approach...?"

"...No, I don't know. What are you looking at me for?"

"No, I mean, are Werebeast chicks into that...?"

"(Are you daft?! I'm as repulsed as you!!)"

"No, hey, let me go! I said, let me gooo!"

Shrieking, the queen somehow managed to shake off Ino's hand.

With that, she turned straight around and vanished with a single stroke of her tail, through the crowd and into the building.

"Please wait, fair queen! Fair queeeeeeeen!!"

Een...een...—een...—...een— Ino's heartrending wail resounded through the sea—and faded. The old man, left in the wake of its echo, drooped brokenly and made no move to leave his place.

—At this sight, all held to their hearts the word *despair*.

"...This is freakin' hopeless."

"......"

—No one refuted Sora's assessment.

"...W-well, he still hasn't been rejected *per se*, right?"

Despite Ino's persistent approach by means of genuflection, the queen still hadn't officially rejected him. Therefore, technically, the game—the dream—should not have been over... To Sora's question, Plum haltingly replied:

"...To begin wiiith, I think the real question is whether you could even consider that a confession of looove..."

Nodding at Plum's words, Sora moved on.

"—'Kay, then why don't we just go on and play normally for now? Command menu...'Leave School,' boop."

"—Huh?"

Reacting to his wide-eyed companions, Sora responded quizzically:

"What? I mean, this is school we're talking about. It's not fun. We'll do our best tomorrow."

"...*Nod, nod.*"

"...You knaves, why'd you make a school the setting, then?"

No one had an answer to the Shrine Maiden's offhanded gripe...

■ DAY 2 ■

When Sora awoke, the "Go to School" command was displayed before him. When he selected the command, his surroundings changed. Before he knew it, he found himself walking to school with Shiro. Everything that led up to this—eating breakfast, changing into his uniform, and leaving the house... All those things had been skipped, yet the memory of doing them lingered vaguely in his head.

"...Brother, good morning..."

"Morning... Hey, I guess we're together from the morning 'cos we're siblings even in the game."

Incidentally, they were also in the same year of school in the game. An eighteen-year-old and an eleven-year-old in the same class—explained away by inferring she'd skipped a lot of grades. As Sora and Shiro headed to school together among the NPCs, a voice announced itself behind them.

"—Oh, Sora. G-good morning to you."

"Hmm...?"

Turning, there stood Steph (in drag). Sora raised a hand to her greeting, and then knitted his brow.

"...Morning. Ya know, it's kinda creepy when you talk like a girl dressed up like that."

"Aren't you the one who went ahead and made it so...?"

Steph, eyes narrowed forbiddingly, produced a thick sheaf of papers from her bag and thrust it before Sora.

"...What is this?"

"It's the queen's profile and contact information in this game. And, also...I did a little digging for some data about the side characters who seem to be her friends at school."

"—What, already?!"

Wide-eyed, Sora flipped through the documentation he'd received. Steph had said "a little," but what he looked through now was documentation covering as many as dozens of characters' info, from phone numbers to hobbies.

—So much info by the second day... Half-appalled at this quick work that would have put the Yoshio to shame, Sora queried:

"Hey, how'd you even dig up this shit?"

Steph stared back blankly before announcing casually:

"It's just like making the rounds in society. All that is required is to draw close a few followers, and everything from interests to grudges to gossip to relationships between the sexes becomes transparent. And it seems that, unlike in the real world, here one can even delve into somewhat personal topics without severing bonds."

——Tsk.

"What?! Why are you tsking at me?!"

Those social skills were fearsome. Though it had been the role he'd expected of her, Steph's social skills were so good that Sora forgot to be grateful and instead just got pissed.

"Never mind, sorry... A-anyway, I'll check it out. Thanks."

Then— Following Sora's recovery and expression of appreciation...

"—U-um, by the way, did that, well...raise your 'Affection'?" Steph (supposed to be a guy in the game) asked, poking her fingers together bashfully.

"...Whaat?"

"Well, you see, I just tried touching the 'Gift'—"

""""**Steeeph! ♪**"""""

"—Agh?!"

Sudden, saccharine voices accosted her from the rear, and Steph pitched forward with a cry. Flustered, she looked back to see a number of girls practically crawling over one another toward her, hearts in their eyes.

"Oh, Steph! Please allow me to go with you to school!"

"Hey, how dare you act so buddy-buddy with him! Oh, come, Steph, please—"

"Wha, hey, I'm still—s-someone save meeeeeee—?!"

Watching Steph dragged off by the throng of schoolgirls, Sora, eyes half-open, said, "......You just go get chased to the end of the world."

He tsked again and went ahead to school, abandoning her.

—When he arrived at school, Ino was still on his hands and knees.

■ DAY 3 ■

Izuna used the "Gift" command on Sora. What she proffered was a can of mackerel. But Izuna was drooling and staring at the can. It seemed she was in the midst of an intense struggle. Sora even started considering going for the Izuna route but just managed to stop himself.

—When he went to school, before the gate, he spotted the queen and Steph. An event? But he hadn't even met them yet, so he ignored the pair and went on to his classroom.

When he got there—she was supposed to be his classmate, apparently—Plum approached him, wearing the girls' uniform.

"U-umm...Why are you all ignoring the queeeen...?"

"'Cos it's easier to earn affection points if you pump up the stats they want first."

"...In the early...game, you skip all the...generic events...and buff your stats for the win..."

At these straight-faced, unanimous assertions from Sora and Shiro, Plum still uneasily inquired:

"...Is that how it worrrks?"

Ino was still at the gate, on his hands and knees.

■ DAY 4 ■

The Shrine Maiden used the "Ask Out" command—on Sora. As he went to school, a voice suddenly called to him, and the Shrine Maiden began.

"I'm a bit interested in this 'cherry coral park' business that's said to be spring-only. Might you accompany me?"

She seemed to be getting this info from the user interface she was examining, but it was news to Sora.

"Huh, what's that? Where'd you find it?"

"What, did it escape your notice? There's a sign like a little book in the lower right."

"Oh, no kidding. *Oceand Journal*—can't believe you got ahead of me in a romance game..."

"Heh-heh-hee... So, what say you? Cherry coral, eh, doesn't it tickle your fancy?"

"Sure, why not. Shiro's down, too, right?"

"...Mm, I'm...curious."

"Why don't we invite the others while we're at it. Izuna, Jibril, Steph—hey, Plum, you in, too?"

"Master, I see 'Make Lunch Box' among my 'Hobby' commands. I shall prepare and bring the fare."

"...Excuse me, you aren't all really forgetting the point of this game, are youuu...?"

Ino was still at the gate, on his hands and knees.

■ DAY 5 ■

It was the day to choose clubs. All unanimously selected the Going-Home Club. Only Steph joined the student council, but for some reason, this was frowned on by the others.

—Leaving school, Shiro tugged at Sora's sleeve. When he looked up—

"...Brother, look."

There was the queen, apparently leaving as well.

"...You can, walk with her...?"

"Probably. But that's a pain in the ass, so let's just go."

"...'If someone, sees us...and gossips...I'd be embarrassed,' right...?"

"My sister, could you please not say that out loud?"

—His memories of the days of his youth were rekindled. That was the line, when you said, "Hey, we're childhood friends. Why not walk home together?"

"Now that I think about it, I kinda have a feeling that was the genesis of my distrust of people."

A restless Plum was saying something to him, but he brushed it off with a *lol, cool story, bro.*

Ino was still at the gate, on his hands and knees.

■ DAY 10 ■

There was an official discussion of the sports day that was supposed to happen the following month. Consensus was that Jibril had it in the bag, and everyone selected the "Leave School" command as soon as they arrived. As he exited the gate, Sora finally gave the date command a try.

—On the Shrine Maiden.

"Uhh, umm, you wanna 'Go Shopping' with everyone?"

"Why do you say it so flatly?"

"Well, it's just one of those obligatory things."

"In any case, is there something droll about going shopping when there's nothing you need?"

"...Looks like, they're having...a gourmet, fair..."

"All right, let's go. They must have sake, eh? Oh, Izuna, will you come along?"

"If they have fish or meat, you don't gotta ask, please."

"Oh, and of course I shall accompany you, Master."

They were going to ask Steph, too, but they didn't see her leaving. Maybe she was busy with the student council.

—They used up all their Money, but they all got to experience some impressive flavors.

Ino was still—you know.

■ DAY 15 ■

"—Hey, why do we even have to go to school at all?"

Prompted by Sora's insight, everyone finally experienced an epiphany. On the heels of it, they quickly concocted a plan to conquer all the date spots they could go to together. Sora and Shiro put in some extra effort and arrived at the spot they'd designated to meet all dressed up, but—

"...Uh, whut...?"

On behalf of the crestfallen Shiro, Sora put it out there.

"...Shrine Maiden... Let me just ask, why are you dressed like that?"

The Shrine Maiden had arrived on the dot in the most unfortunate attire of a tracksuit and sandals. In her getup, like some dopey dad lounging around the house, the Shrine Maiden raised her hands in explanation.

"They didn't have a *hakama* or *waraji*. These aren't much to look at, but they're comfortable to move in. Look at yourselves; isn't it a little queer to go hiking in a suit and a dress?"

"I would also like to ask Jibril why she is wearing a swimsuit."

"What? A selection of clothing arose, and I simply selected that which most resembled my usual attire."

...By the way, according to Steph, who was still going to school like a good girl, Ino was, after all this, you know.

■ DAY 20 ■

—They were all finally starting to get bored. For a change of pace, everyone decided to actually go to school. When they arrived, for some reason, there was some rumor going around that Sora had hurt (male) Steph's feelings. After tracking Steph down at lunch to ask what the hell was going on—

"......!"

As soon as she saw Sora's face, Steph grimly changed color and bolted.

"What's this all about?"

"...That's just...how the, game works..."

Getting the bomb symbol for doing nothing was, yeah, the design. But why was there one on—a guy (in in-game terms)?

"Hey, Plum, this game's engine is broken."

"...More importantlyyy, you really have forgotten the point of the game, haven't youuu?"

Sora objected, *Debug your damn game*, but Plum just sighed sadly with distant eyes.

—Meanwhile—Ino. Still at the gate. Hands and knees...—

DAY 25

Nothing special happened. It was starting to look like an end of a summer journal.

■ DAY 30 ■

Nothing special.

DAY 35

Nothing, etc.

■ DAY 39 ■

—Why not try going to school tomorrow? After all, by now you did have to wonder how Ino was doing—

■ DAY 40 ■

—The morning glow painted the sky. In front of the illuminated gate, there was a statue, gaunt and covered in barnacles, fused to the ground. This monument that exuded the impression of being some sort of solemn sacrament—
    "...N-no way... Is this, Gramps?"
    —made the party, after returning to school following a long absence, hold their collective breath.

    —Even Sora and the rest, all of whom had cringed at Ino's display...now found themselves at a loss for words. The figure that seemed on the verge of being encircled by a halo was—unmistakably and above all else—manly.
    ...Since the day the game began, that stolid figure had continued his vigil of genuflection before the queen, who every day passed silently

by before him. Like a statue, without so much as a twitch. And now it had come to this. There were no words for it. No, more accurately, this form itself said it all eloquently, loud and clear. That is—

Give it to me, baby——!!

At the noble figure before him, Sora, as a fellow man, had no choice but to respectfully admit the truth. *I see now... Romance is not a mind game.*

—It is a demonstration of love. The old man embodied his own words. In which case—Sora was more than convinced that he himself had no conception of true love. Sora—staggering to the statue— no, the man—trembled.

"How small—how very small I've been," Sora whispered as he compared himself with this paragon. For his own love—so petty, it must be said—could he remain fixed to the earth for forty days? Sora could only answer no. But this man, Ino, had done just that. Without distorting who he was, without fear of shame, he pounded on a heart exposed for all to see. Could there be a truer love than this—? There could not!

"I see... This, this is love, true love..."

"...In, your...dreams..."

Shiro promptly smacked down the near tearful epiphany suggested by Sora's muttering. But—suddenly. Upon that sacred statue. Obscuring the morning sun—a shadow was cast. Tracing the shadow back to its owner, who slid elegantly through the water on her way to school—there was—the queen herself. Her gaze cut right past Sora to the sacred image—no, to Ino—stared.

—Could it be?

"...You jest—could it possibly be...?" The Shrine Maiden, who had been watching from a distance, couldn't help but whisper. But the queen edged forward, still closer to Ino, and placed her hands softly upon his cheeks. At that moment...the statue moved as if at long last remembering it was alive. The barnacles, the earth, the caked stone sloughed off. Guided by the queen's softly applied hands, Ino's face rose. And—with that voice that enraptured all who heard it, with a smile more beautiful than all the treasures of the world—she spoke.

"…No way."

—*Ah, of course…* The hearts of all echoed harmoniously.
"—Ngkh…"
But Ino gritted his teeth as if to say, *it's not over yet.* It was true—his love had been rebuffed. He had eroded heroically, to dust. But—in this of all times, he had only one choice—! To fulfill the duty with which the Shrine Maiden had charged him—Ino selected a command from the UI.
—The heart icon with a plus. In other words—Plum's cheat command. And—
"—Forgive me, O Queen! Hrm, nghhhhhhrrrrrr!!"
Soundly and with the power of a grappling sumo wrestler…
…he squeezed the queen's breast. Yes—he executed the command to complete Plum's rite.
"——Wha?!"
Instantly, red light swirled around the queen, and her eyes opened wide.
—In the same instant…
"—Ah, ghk—!"
A complex pattern etched itself in Plum's retinas, and she released a strangled cry. Her power perhaps having been seized all at once, her black wings for a moment turned the color of blood, and then she fell to sit on the ground.

"…Ah, ahh…"
But the queen, her breast still in Ino's grasp, raised a thin voice. Her face flushed vermilion—and even Sora and the others could see that her heart was pounding.
"We—we did it— Now—!"
Even Plum announced confidently, "N-nowww, however much Mr. Ino may be a creep who thinks with his nether regions,

regardless of what emotion the queen experiences as a resulllt... she'll interpret it—as having fallen in looove!" Plum took advantage of the chaos to speak her mind, but she still sounded tired.

Even Sora thought it was a really twisted spell. But by whatever means, in the end, the queen was "in love." Which meant the game was over.

—And then.

"—No, no-no-no. Fall in love with him? Yeah, right. Not happening. Sorry!!"

—Thus decisively rejecting Ino, the queen—as if flying—headed for school with a flap of her tail.

...

——......

...*Saaadneeess*...—A bit of background music in that vein played through Sora's mind. The man had burned out. Burned white—well, he'd always been a ball of white fur, but—pure white. The interface displayed the words: Ino Hatsuse: Defeated. But before the gate, having gone down—still, still—having burned out, but even still...

—His figure still holding the posture in which he had squeezed the queen's breast—Ino Hatsuse had turned to ash. Reeling...Sora approached. He could not find the words.

—But, even so, he had to say it.

"Old far—I mean...Ino Hatsuse. I had you wrong." Voice quivering, Sora searched for the proper eulogy. "You're the real thing...a big—man. Too big for her...a woman with no eyes..."

However, Ino, as if on the verge of turning completely to ash and disappearing, even so, he managed a reply.

"—No, King Sora... It was that my love was not enough. Love is no crime."

With these words—rejected, his rights stripped from him as he was ejected from the game—Ino gradually faded from the color of ash to become transparent—and then—

"Ino...? Ino, hey, hold on! No way?!"

Unaffected by Sora's cry as Immanity's king put his arm around Ino's shoulder, the old man's body vanished from the game.

—With that, the curtain fell on the high school career of Ino Hatsuse—a life seemingly so full but, in reality, composed entirely of genuflection. If he could do it once more…this time, he would leave no…

…It would be typical to leave some wussy lines like that at the end.

"Heh…I have no regrets… If I could do it again, I would do the same—" With a self-satisfied smile, Ino instead decisively repudiated such introspection and vanished from Sora's arms.

—In the dead silence that lingered, Sora looked to the sky. Wetting his manly cheeks with tears.

"Ino Hatsuse—how could you be so—ngkh!"

Despite Sora's one-man show, everyone else looked on coolly.

—It wasn't even worth chills. Ino wasn't dead; he hadn't even really vanished. He'd just been sent back outside the game. But Sora, as if having lost an irreplaceable brother in arms, trembled.

"What…is this—?!"

Sora shrieked at Plum, her eyes as disengaged as the others, as if about to cough blood.

"What is this?! Didn't you say it was a sure win?! That man went as far as to sacrifice his own sensibility!! He went as far as to use a 'cheat' for you guys, so why…?! Why—didn't the queen let him put it iiin?!!"

"—Uh, welll…you see, even with magic, do you really expeeect…?"

Plum's muttered reply was actually quite reasonable. The same thought had floated through the back of the Shrine Maiden's mind. It seemed more realistic to fall in love with some rock than with *that. Still—*…she thought. Regardless of the Shrine Maiden and her thin smile, Sora, on his knees, pounded the ground and raged.

"Don't screw with me! Could there be any more of a man than that—?! *I'm right, aren't I? Shiro, Shrine Maiden, Jibril?!*"

Responding to the voice that howled at them, the three whose names had been called just—

—*nodded.*

"…Wha-whaaaa?"
Steph winced back a step.
Meanwhile, squirming under Sora's unbearable glare and flustered, Plum chided, "P-please calm dowwwn… Th-this was just an extreme caaase… We can retrieve Mr. Ino from Her Highness Amila, and, if you will just play normally *once more*, Sirrr…"
With these words, peering into Sora's face, Plum—

"—…?!"
—felt her heart snatched and squashed. Or rather, the illusion of it. Before her—the Sora who had been there previously was no more. The man who had just been raging, raising his voice, swinging his arms, was no more. The man who had smiled frivolously as he listened to Plum's request, the rake, was no more. The man crouching there—was *someone Plum didn't know.* Wearing an insolently thin smile… A man with the eyes of a hunter pitying the prey that had fallen into his trap. This man, in a voice that chilled to the bone, said only this:

"Once more? —What for?"
—After all…
"We've, already…won…"

"—Huh…?"
It was Shiro who finished the thought of the man who slowly rose, his eyes devoid of the slightest warmth. And Shiro, too…had become a stranger to Plum. Her eyes were at absolute zero. Plum fell back a step at this transformation. She didn't know these two. But Steph, Jibril, the Shrine Maiden, and Izuna…did. The only ones who

tragically didn't know these siblings—Sora and Shiro—were Plum and her cohort who of all people *had made them an enemy.* Standing before her with that bearing they had when they'd sprung a trap with no margin for escape—

—was the worst of enemies: " ".

"—That should be enough, right, Shrine Maiden, Jibril?" Sora asked, veering to face them.

"Aye, I've had my fill of fun. *You can do it now.*"

"I have obtained confirmation. I am ready—*at your command.*"

At the affirmations of the pair, Sora commanded hollowly:

"Knock yourself out, Jibril."

"—As you wish."

Thus bowing once, Jibril opened her wings.

—And with that, the rite constructed through the cooperation of dozens of Dhampirs—the game that meddled in the queen's very dreams—was scattered as easily as the seeds of a dandelion as the group's surroundings shattered.

⏻ CHAPTER 4
WILD CARD
THE FOOL

—Space exploded. A shock reverberated such that Amila, watching the game from outside, could only react thusly:

"…Huh?"

—Greeting the party as the dream world ruptured and they awoke were Plum and Amila, their eyes wide. The rite Plum had woven with dozens of assistants, even supplied as they had been with blood, had been pulverized with one simple gesture of Jibril's will— but that wasn't what left them stunned. That was a consequence of Sora's declaration as he rose.

"—Yo, *check*. Looks like we win."

"…Uh, umm, Amila doesn't really get what's going ooon! Uhh?"

Sora and Shiro replied, casually and briefly, to Amila's tense smile, and for the edification of everyone else listening.

"…We 'saved and exited'…you…*didn't say we couldn't…*"

"No one said we couldn't leave the game before we were all

rejected. So we can *exit the game no problem*, yeah...? You gotta remember to set out covenant language carefully, you know?"

Disinterestedly filling in the entourage as they rose, Sora continued.

"All right, Jibril, go ahead. *Bring back the air.*"

"—At your command."

Immediately, Jibril nonchalantly traced a magical path with her finger.

—And suddenly, a gale assailed the queen's chamber. In a matter of moments, the water was repelled, and the chamber of the queen— filled with air.

"...Huh...?"

Jibril smirked at the dazed Plum and Amila. "Pardon me... I simply restored the air I brought along with me, *compressed as a bubble.*"

In the large hall, the water splashed about as it was pushed away and the air took its place.

"——Kh-*hhh...hh*—...hff...huh, huh-huh..."

—Having until now *remained utterly silent except in the dream*, the Shrine Maiden, who'd thus far kept a mask of composure, warped her expression. Heaving her shoulders at *finally* being able to breathe, she laughed.

Her body instantly turned red, raising a steam of evaporated blood.

—She then casually divulged the secret.

"Bearing up against *twenty atmospheres* of water pressure for such a long time by *brute force*... Even with my bloodbreak, it's too much."

The Shrine Maiden, seemingly about to collapse in the recoil of the unreasonable strain that had just been lifted from her, but somehow stubbornly managing to stop at sitting cross-legged instead, sneered with her chin in her hand.

"——Huh?"

Plum, Amila—and Steph all looked baffled. But, with no sign of engaging with them, Sora continued, all emotion falling from his expression as if it had been just a mask.

"—But to think, with that much water pressure, your blood won't leave your body—that let you use your bloodbreak without leaving a trace for these guys to *catch on that you were reading their minds to your heart's content the whole time*—nice job, Shrine Maiden. So what'd you find out?"

Seeing his face—

"...You surely know how to throw your weight around, don't you...? All right, why not."

—the Shrine Maiden smirked, as from her heart she was glad he was on her side.

"That Siren there—*has no mind to wake the queen at all.*"

—At this accusation, Amila's expression clearly wavered, and at the words that followed, delivered with a tone of *and not only that...* she now clearly froze.

"What they came up with to be your *bait*—the 'ante' the queen put up—was *malarkey as well*—goodness gracious."

Soothed by Amila's and Plum's reactions, the Shrine Maiden smiled as if embarrassed and continued to Sora with kind eyes.

"And that business about you being her type or handsome or somesuch, likewise *all malarkey.*"

"Well, yeah, I figured that much—. ...God damn it."

The Shrine Maiden beamed merrily at Sora's vexation. And—as if mocking Amila and Plum—"...Did you think my senses *would be dulled under the sea?*"

She acted almost embarrassed, yet with her face warped into the most scornful of sneers.

"—Let me tell you, it's no idle boast or drunken rave when it's said I'm the strongest among Werebeast."

Struggling not to let on he'd been hurt, Sora averted his eyes.

"Yes, Master. I can also say this without doubt." Picking up his gaze, Jibril lowered herself reverently before her king and declared:

"The rite woven by Plum activated properly, precisely, to win the queen's love just as it should have."

This time it was Plum's turn to freeze.

"—Without a doubt, it *operated flawlessly, and the queen has received its effects properly.*"

Sora silently considered the possibility that it had been faked, but Jibril answered that with a smile. "Fear not. *This is the very reason we tested it on the Shrine Maiden first*, is it not?"

Smiling back, Sora said *finally*—and turned to Shiro. But there was nothing more that needed to be said.

"…Mm…I got it all…down…"

—With these few words, Shiro answered all of her brother's expectations. As if satisfied with every response, Sora nodded once. He wore his usual frivolous grin, but over that smile was the shadow cast by his bangs and the too-sharp light of his eyes. The combination was a convincing replication of a fierce glare as he spoke.

"—Hey, you guys. *Did you really think you could eat us for lunch?*"

Plum's and Amila's eyes faintly quivered at this accusation. If they thought that, of all people, Sora would be unable to read such a tell as a bull's-eye—that would be just—

"Uh, uh, um, wh-what are you talking about?"

"……?"

Steph and Izuna didn't seem to get what was going on. They looked back and forth, bemused. But, as if he had no intention of explaining further, Sora clapped his hands together and turned away.

"Okay, let's go, Jibril. Back to the beach."

"As you wish."

As Jibril spread her wings and spun her halo, they all hurried to touch her.

"Uh, excuse meee! P-pleaase waiiit!"

As Plum likewise hurried to their side—

"Good call, Dhampir. You're done playing the pitiful victim?"

—Sora's thin smirk as he waited for her sent a cold jolt down her spine. Amila spoke up.

"Whaaat? What about Mr. Inooo; we still 'have' him, you knowww? I wonder if you should really be going home alreadyyy. ♥"

Gazes collected at the spot by Amila's feet where Ino lay sprawled. Izuna's gaze nervously flickered between Ino and Team Sora.

"Yeah, sure we can," Sora said smoothly. "'Cos, dude…*you know what happens if you lay a finger on him—don't you*?"

Looking back at Amila's widening eyes, Sora sneered mockingly. "You think you can *play dumb* in front of me—? Never underestimate that which you should fear, *noob*."

And turning his back to her:

"*—We'll be back*, Siren. Underestimating us is gonna cost you."

Then, by means of Jibril's teleportation, all except Amila and Ino disappeared.

■■■

The party found itself once more on the shore. The sun had long since set, and the red moon and countless stars—along with a bonfire—were all that lit the beach. The waves and the sparks from the fire, too, were the only sounds as Sora & Co. conspired merrily.

"Oh, Shiro, looks pretty much done, huh?"

"…Tropical fish…you can eat them…?"

"It is a fish of the sea known as 'rerité.' I understand that the flavor is quite palatable."

—All having been teleported by Jibril from Oceand to the beach—and inadvertently carrying a large seawater haul in their wake, Sora and crew now busied themselves cooking it on the beach.

"*Hwaahh*—. …Just the thing with some sake after a job well done… While we're at it—" The Shrine Maiden knocked back her cup.

"While we're at it—we might as well have sliced and fried some tofu—you mean?"

"—How did you know I like *abura-age*? Did I tell you?"

Sora and Shiro laughed at the Shrine Maiden's bemusement. One step away from this pleasant and peaceful scene—

"What—what is this…? What is the meaning of this?" Steph shrieked dubiously, not seeming to fathom the situation at all. Beside her, Izuna looked down wordlessly. And, a little farther on yet, lingered Plum, also silent.

Casting Steph a glance and biting into his roast fish, Sora said, "Nothing in particular—it's just *Plum tried to play us*. That's all."

As if to answer Steph's wide-eyed glare at Plum, he added:

"When did we figure it out, you ask? Hey, Plum."

Now addressing Plum as she lowered her face, Sora continued with a snicker. Plum looked up fearfully, but Sora went on, grinning casually.

"From the start—your story was *fishy through and through*."

Taking his lead, Shiro, the Shrine Maiden, and Jibril smirked.

—All right, Dhampir and Siren were in a symbiotic relationship. It broke down when the queen went to sleep, and now they were on the brink of doom. Plum had had no argument with Jibril's assessment—but. Grinning as if having heard a cheesy joke, Sora chuckled.

"'We made a spell that can wake her up for sure; help us'—ha-ha, *yeah, right*."

"...Huh? Wh-what do you mean?"

Steph seemed lost, so Sora proffered a stick of roast fish. "Wouldn't it be way more appetizing to *lie* that you had a sure win, sucker 'em into an impossible game, and chow down?"

"——......"

Hearing Sora's smiling pronouncement of this sick notion, Steph's face contorted independently of her will.

"—Having said that, there were a few things that got to me."

Stuffing his face with fish, Sora continued.

"It didn't look to me like Plum was lying. We even had Izuna in the same room, and she didn't seem to catch on to anything—oh, hey, that's right. Izuna, don't you want fish?"

Remembering the night they first met Plum, Izuna rebuffed the stick Sora extended—

"......No thanks, please."

Standing at a slight distance, Izuna shook her head minutely. Across from her, the Shrine Maiden, downing her sake, also closed her eyes and shook her head.

"Yeah, that's why we took her to the Shrine Maiden's place, too, just to be safe—and *she wasn't lying after all*."

Given that Jibril was on guard, any magic spells or such to camouflage a lie would have been seen through. In which case, it was assumed that before the Shrine Maiden, strongest among Were-beast, any lie would be sniffed out for certain. But—he went on, steadily applying a fish to the flame—"And then what Plum showed us, if can you believe it, really was a spell that could make someone fall in love for sure."

Lit by the bonfire, Sora followed his train of thought, somehow seeming amused even as his smile swayed creepily.

"So if she really had a sure win—then why ask us for help?"

"Wh-what you're saying, basically, is that she wasn't lying, isn't it?"

Wouldn't that mean that she just genuinely wanted their help—? Fiddling with the skewer in his hand, Sora tackled Steph's query:

"Right, she wasn't lying—and therein lies the problem."

—Sora dropped his gaze to Shiro curled up at his knees, who picked up the explanation for him:

"...June 20, 22:42 UTC... Brother..." Just like a recorder, word for word—

"...'And *what do we get* if we win this game?'..."

Following the Coordinated Universal Time of their old world based on her phone—remembering everything down to the time-line and intonation—Shiro reproduced Sora's words with the precision of replay, and everyone stared.

"—And what was it again that Plum said after I asked that?"

"...June 20, 22:43 UTC... Plum..." Expressionlessly, calmly. "...'Um...We'll guarantee you thirty percent of Oceand's marine resources, and friendly relations for perpetuityyy...! ...A-and also...uhh... Y-you can do anything you want with meee'..."

Sora smiled bashfully at Shiro's "rewind" of Plum's offer.

"Right—this is it. She wasn't lying—but she wasn't telling the truth, either."

Sora took the stick he'd been playing with and thrust it in Steph's direction.

"Steph, when they said we had to bet everything on their game, you were all in our faces, right?"

"Uh, yes... For they were the ones who requested help, weren't they?"

"Yeah, *you were right.*"

"—Uh, what?"

Announcing it placidly, Sora went on shamelessly as he bit into his fish.

"I said you were wrong just to get them to spill what we needed to know. Let me make it up to you by revealing what it is that was nagging at you."

That thing that had been nagging at her...a fear she couldn't express except a certainty that something was off.

"This game, you know—*it's like a horse race.*"

"A—a horse race? You mean, like gambling?"

Sora, nodding in his mind, *I'm glad to hear they gamble on horse races in this world, too.*

"A horse race is a game where people gamble on which horse will win... But the core contest is still *the race itself*—the rivalry among the riders."

To put it simply:

"A horse race—is a game of chance based on a challenge among the jockeys—it's a *double game.*"

"We were the riders racing for the queen's love."

But—

"Meanwhile, the promises Amila and Plum made of marine resources and friendly relations were just the payout on our bet on the queen waking up. The racing and the gambling are supposed to be two separate games, yet they had us playing as both the horses and the gamblers—of course that's fishy."

...*Oh.* Steph took a sharp, surprised breath. Following along with Sora's analogy, they were the racers themselves, and yet... *They were prompted to stake it all by wagering on themselves*—made to participate in both games.

But Sora, as if reading Steph's thoughts, shook his head. "That's not even the problem.

"So, if we say this is a horse race, what about us as racers—*Where's our prize money?*"

With a wicked smile, he cast a look at Plum.

"Um, i-isn't it the queen's love...the queen waking up?"

"—If you make me fall in love with you, I'll fall in love with you? She'll wake up for the sake of the prince she loves? —First, that's total bullshit, and, second, *the queen comes out ahead either way, doesn't she*? What happened to the 'wager of equal value' for the victor?"

Finally, Steph arrived at the source of her misgivings. The marine resources, the friendly relations, domination over Plum—none of these things seemed like things the queen would have specified. In that case, the queen's wager in the game she'd sworn by the Covenants before sleeping... The reward she'd figured was of equal value—to be paid to the rider who won—

—the prize money—

——*hadn't been mentioned at all?!*

The Shrine Maiden grinned slyly and played with the stick that had held the fish she'd just eaten.

"'Tis a set of games with two sides. But when Mr. Sora brought up what he stood to gain from winning the game, that Dhampir there answered *deliberately so as not to touch on that two-sidedness*. She told no lie." *But*—smiled the Shrine Maiden. "What is not a lie—*still may not be the truth.*"

Hearing that bull's-eye noise coming from. Plum's heart as this truth was laid down, the Shrine Maiden smirked. Sora, though, with an exaggerated performance of deep thought—

"So, here's the problem... Why *didn't she mention the two-sidedness*?"

Playing with his stick, Sora turned to Plum.

"Until we were underwater—where you *thought* the Shrine Maiden's and Izuna's senses would be cut off—you didn't bring it up. Why couldn't you just have told us something as simple as, 'Amila says it's no-risk'?"

Positioned behind Sora, Jibril diligently occupied herself with chopping up fish, sticking it on skewers, and seasoning it. Handing a well-salted piece of fish on a stick to him, she offered, "—For speaking these words would constitute a lie...I presume."

With a thin smile, she answered his question. Sora nodded to Shiro as if to say, *which means...*

"—...June 20, 04:28 UTC... Plum... 'Please save our raaace!'..."

Nibbling at her fish like a rodent, Shiro deftly rendered Plum's— —first line in "playback."

"If this *isn't a lie*, that means she wanted us to save their race—that is, Dhampir."

Which meant—

"She wanted us to save Dhampir—*only*—so then *what's the methodology?*"

As Steph was incapable of responding to his rhetoric save to round her eyes like glass ornaments, he ignored her. He took the stick with which he'd been toying—and tossed it onto the sand next to where Plum was seatecd.

"So, now we've got everything we need to figure it out, right?"

One—and another, throwing additional sticks in the same manner.

"The questions are three. The conclusion is one."

Casting his eyes upon the beach where the three sticks protruded from the sand, Sora gave her the setup.

"—You ready for this, Plum?"

As if in response to Sora's pronouncement, in the light only of the fire, the red moon, and the stars, four pairs of eyes glinted, each with its own variety of light.

The first to move was the Shrine Maiden.

"—Why is it that you shied from mentioning matters relating to the two-sided nature of the game?"

The stick launched by the Shrine Maiden whooshed through the wind and caught Sora's first—splitting it in two.

"Because she couldn't lie."

Hearing Sora's answer, the next to move was Jibril.

"Whyever would you request our help when you already have a spell that will make her fall in love?"

Jibril's wooden projectile made a sonic boom and caught Sora's second skewer, shattering it.

"Because *Plum* couldn't lie."

At Sora's response, the last to move was Shiro.

"...In the first place...why—*couldn't*...she lie?"

Shiro's skewer arced through the air and caught the core of Sora's third—and stuck there.

"Because if she lied—*we'd know.*"

—Indeed.

"If it's a horse race, then you gotta remember—everyone's betting on *different horses.*"

Amila was betting on—the queen. Plum was betting on—Team Sora. Two games. Two wills. And, taking all of this into account, there was indeed but one conclusion.

"Siren was using the sleeping queen game as bait to chow down on Immanity."

"Wha——!"

Steph alone was still shocked. Siren, just as Sora had said at the beginning, had made the game out to be cake to draw in Sora and Shiro—the agent plenipotentiary of Immanity. To avert the destruction of their race by gaining new "resources for reproduction"—Immanity itself. But—

"Dhampir took it a step farther and plotted against Siren—to stab them in the back and free Dhampir."

Yes—Plum was *actually* trying to make the queen fall in love. But Amila—wasn't.

"So she couldn't lie around Werebeasts, but *she couldn't tell the truth that there were two agendas, either.*"

As usual, Steph alone was speechless, just flabbergasted. But— Sora raised his hand to say, *Hold on.*

—To say, *This is where it gets good.*

"So, let's think back, shall we? What's the prize money for winning the queen's game?"

Tossing a merry smile at Plum, Sora turned his line of sight. And—under the moon, glinting sharp, four pairs of eyes shone.

"Be there aught to make Amila—to make Siren—prefer to maintain the status quo rather than awaken the queen?"

The Shrine Maiden, with her bewitching golden eyes, smirked.

"Whatever could make Plum—could make Dhampir—believe that emancipation lay before their eyes to seize?"

And Jibril, with her inorganic amber eyes, sneered.

"...Something that threatens the existence of Siren...and would allow Dhampir...to reclaim their rights..."

And Shiro, with her emotionless ruby eyes, simpered. And, taking each of these sequential observations was Sora, with his obsidian eyes. Coldly he brought them all together.

"The queen's wager was—*'everything I have'*...right?"

—Plum hung her head, and Steph took a breath. While the current queen had slept. She wasn't quite queen—wasn't quite the agent plenipotentiary. But now things were different. Now, if the victory conditions for her wager were fulfilled—it would mean everything Siren was.

—Literally everything, even the Race Piece, would go to the victor. But, ignoring Steph as she shivered, Sora continued to grin his coy grin—and dropped a few words that made Steph doubt her ears.

"This much we figured out *before coming to the beach*."

"—Huh?"

"But, still...we couldn't say we had proof. So that's why we decided to head for Oceand."

As if to confirm it—but in a teasing tone, Sora laid it all out.

"It was the *beach*, after all. I got my fun in—in other words..."

Then, after giving Plum the sickest smile of all, in a single breath—he revealed the answers to all of the remaining secrets—rapid-fire.

"Shiro and I:

- Dragged you out to the beach in the blazing sun to sap your power
- Had the Shrine Maiden pretend to mess around with Jibril while actually verifying that she could cover up her bloodbreak with water pressure
- Simultaneously had Jibril go way out into the ocean to check where Oceand was

- Gave the Shrine Maiden time to recover from her bloodbreak while Shiro helped her by petting her till night came
- Skipped out on your welcome boat, that was probably a trap, and had Jibril warp us in
- Created a situation in which you had to get blood from Siren to cast your underwater breathing spell on us
- Made you leave while Jibril compressed and stored the air she'd brought
- Then had Jibril jam your underwater breathing spell so it wouldn't work on the Shrine Maiden
- And met Amila with the ability to utilize Werebeast's senses to their fullest even at the bottom of the sea

—So, yeah. Didja figure it out?"

...

......——

—Both Plum and Steph were just totally dumbfounded, unable to speak. But, seemingly unconcerned, Sora just checked to see if his fish was done and said:

"You had no way to get all the way to the game without lying. 'Cos you had to get us to wager 'everything' by the Covenants. To uncover your lie, the Shrine Maiden had to be free of your fishy magic."

A spell that enabled breathing and conversation underwater— cast, of all people, by Plum, who they knew was their enemy—was likely to fool their senses. Having laid it all out, Sora continued.

"Siren and Dhampir each bet on different horses—but did you forget? It was you who got us to put down everything on our own tickets and participate in both the race and the gambling—*we've got tickets, too.*"

—Indeed.

"——Tickets on *us getting ahead of all of you and winning.*

"Man, I gotta hand it to you, Plum. That was an awesome strategy from a weak position. That's how a race thinks when it's got all its power owned by the Ten Covenants. I mean, that way, Dhampir would still get an extra life if Amila got her way and chomped up Immanity, while, if we actually did manage to wake up the queen and Siren—"

From his heart, without irony, Sora clapped his hands in praise.

"She'd be in love because of *your spell, not us*, so you'd run away with the lot."

—Having casually called out the reason Plum had participated in the game, Sora continued.

"Look, I'm not the kind of guy to flatter people, so I mean it when I say this—that is a sweet strategy."

To create a situation in which she would win wherever the chips fell, while having to do almost nothing herself, instead getting other people to do it for her and walking off with the rewards. Now that was truly the ideal way to win. But—

"I think there's something you're overlooking."

"—Huh?"

With this, Plum raised her downcast head.

"Don't you get it? The point isn't that we just totally blew your cover. It's not that you were hiding the prize money for winning the queen's game in a plot to emancipate your race, either. You couldn't wake up the queen even with a spell you had total confidence would work—*but that's not even it.*"

—And, then, twisting his face. With the most ironic of tones, Sora spoke.

"It's that Amila is assuming there's not one chance in a million we'll wake the queen."

"——…Oh—"

Plum's breath stopped. Yes, because that explained everything. Why Ino hadn't been able to beat the game—Plum's spell had activated properly. It had worked on the queen, without a doubt, Jibril had said as much. Yet, even so, she hadn't awakened.

Which meant——

"The condition to wake up the queen—*isn't to make her fall in love.*"

—...*Grsh.* Though Plum's molars ground audibly, still Sora continued.

"*Amila knew that.* If she hadn't, no matter how much you enticed her, she'd never have given you a chance to possibly wake up the queen. It would be fatal for Siren—you see?"

Sora now dropped even his scornful smile.

"Amila, of whom you thought so little—took your betrayal *into account.*"

"...—!"

Yet—Sora rained down another blow upon Plum as she sat on the beach, outstripped even by Siren, of whom she'd thought nothing at all.

"That's a hell of a strategy for the weak, a really slick play—but it ain't the real thing."

Indeed. The wisdom of the weak could not be wielded to its full potential by the strong. For what formed its foundation...

...was the cowardice borne of abject weakness.

Sora finally flipped off his smile and spoke with a serious mien.

"The natural enemy of the strong is the weak, but the natural enemy of the weak isn't the strong—it's the *weaker.*"

The weak—the man who embodied this word advanced intimidatingly on Plum. Squatting to eye level with the seated Dhampir, he softly and directly announced:

"A fool who knows what he is, is far more fearsome than a fool who thinks he's smart."

Without touching on who he was just talking about, Sora moved on:

"So—it's *check.*"

Plum blanched. To begin with, the only ones who had accepted these conditions were *Sora & Co.* But now that they'd laid everything bare and left the game, she was out of options. That meant that all Siren could do to survive was to devour the last male to whom Dhampir so desperately clung. Now that Plum's betrayal had been confirmed, it was all the more likely Siren would do precisely that.

—So Dhampir was pretty much screwed. But, then, if Dhampir died, Siren would be next. Siren—would have to find someone to give them permission to procreate. But who would say yes to these broads who demanded your death to reproduce?

—Whence it followed that Siren was also screwed. The only way they could survive would be unconditional surrender—being *turned into livestock.*

"—Plum, do you know the ultimate way to win a game?"

A chilling, devilish smile.

"—*By default.* We don't even have to beat the queen's game for this to be *our win.*"

Dragging Plum down to the depths of hell—with a smile.

"You think you can beat the weakest with the tactics of the weak, you got another thing comin'—ya friggin' n00bs."

—One move. In just one move, having seized the power of life and death over two races. Darkly, he smiled and spoke.

"So, I hope you get the gist of the situation. By the way..."

Sora now fidgeted as if uneasy. And, if you looked carefully, Shiro, enshrined on his lap, also seemed to be writhing—

"Oh, dear... Master, what is it?"

......

"—Wh-where's the bathroom?" Sora inquired with a piteous visage that reduced the rarefied atmosphere of a moment ago to rubble.

"Bathroom...oh, you mean the chambers Immanities use to urinate and—"

"What else would I mean?!"

Then suddenly thrusting his finger individually everyone at around, Sora shrieked.

"I mean, what kind of bladders do all you guys have?! After a full day at the beach and then going to the bottom of the sea and then coming back to the beach at night and eating fish and shit, who the hell can last that long?!"

"...B-Brother...I-I...have to go, too...!"

The Shrine Maiden laughed superciliously at Shiro as he pleaded with teary eyes. "No beauty does such things. I can't say I know how it feels, but why don't you go do your business wherever serves?"

—*Jibril's one thing, but you're a "living thing," aren't you?*—he would've said. But apparently not even having the time for quips like that, Sora rose.

"O-okay, we're—I mean, I'm going to the bathroom. Shiro's going to pick flowers!"

Sora, snatching up Shiro and dashing off.

"...B-Brother—d-don't...shake...meee..."

"Aagh, this is the beach! They've gotta have one of those beach shacks! Where is it?!"

With Sora and Shiro's noisy departure, all that remained was the still beach.

——......The waves and the crackling of the fire were the only sounds.

"And so, all we've left to do is to wait for their unconditional surrender, eh. I'm a bit weary. I'll be taking my leave."

With these words, the Shrine Maiden stood wearily and turned—

"H-hey, hold on, you! What about Mr. Ino!"

—only to have Steph descend on her, having finally caught up with the situation.

—All right, she'd understood that Siren meant to gobble up Immanity. She grasped that Plum had plotted to exploit this for the emancipation of Dhampir. She saw that Sora and Shiro had seen through it all and gone another step ahead. But still—Siren held the Ino Hatsuse card. That was one question that was still unresolved, ranted Steph. The Shrine Maiden paused, looking back. With a smile even more bewitching for the light of the moon—eerie as a specter's—she spoke.

"*There is naught for it.* 'Tis enough to bring two races into our hands—a fine bargain, wouldn't you say?"

At the Shrine Maiden's assertion that there was no trump card, Steph finally understood it all. So—to sum up: Neither Sora, nor

Shiro, nor the Shrine Maiden *ever had any intention of saving him*—!
The three of them had colluded—to make this one move that would
trap two races. For this. Just for this. As if it were nothing.

—They'd *sacrificed Ino*—!

"…That…I cannot tolerate."

"Hmm?"

While almost overwhelmed by those golden, literally inhuman
eyes of a raptor, still—somehow—Steph looked around and managed to squeeze out her voice. Ino Hatsuse—the Werebeast who had
been the only one to support Steph in Elkia when Sora and Shiro
were away—albeit only for two weeks. He'd played alongside her,
even fought to rebuild Elkia alongside her. He'd done so much to
lay the foundations for the Commonwealth of Elkia; without him,
she'd have had no ground under her feet. For the Eastern Union and
for Elkia—for Steph!—he was an intrinsically valuable asset, and,
on top of that, to make a sacrifice a member of just one race while
attempting to bring together two… The risk of such an action was
incalculable. It was so self-evident, it defied comprehension that the
Shrine Maiden wouldn't understand—

"Ino Hatsuse. There was a man of ability, who held me strong,
right from the early days of the Eastern Union. A man who would
accept an order to die for the Eastern Union with an 'As you
wish'—indeed a credit to his people—and now he's demonstrated
his mighty prowess to the very end. What could one possibly say
against such a man?"

The Shrine Maiden spoke, gazing longingly up at the moon. If
even she would be so calculating as to toss him away as if he was
nothing—! (Does that not mean that *I, too, could be cast aside at any
time*—?! Who could trust one such as that?!)

While Steph raged, Izuna, who'd been sitting apart the whole
time, suddenly appeared in her field of vision.

—Of course. It was inconceivable that Izuna could accept this situation. Her own grandfather had just been sacrificed. If she thought
anything of Izuna, even the Shrine Maiden would have to—

"M-Miss Izuna, do you—"

—*accept this?* Steph was going to ask, but Izuna's manner as she sat apart, holding her knees as if resisting something, made Steph choke back her words. It was hard to see her in the darkness, but— the Werebeast mumbled.

"...Grampy knew what he was doing, the asshole, please..."

Away from the fire, lit only by the moon and stars, Izuna's expression was invisible.

"...Grampy's heartbeat, his smell...to the end, he sounded good, he smelled good...the asshole, please."

Yet Izuna's quivering voice, her wet words—even in the darkness of the beach—revealed her expression all too vividly.

"I don't want lose Grampy, please... But I'm the only asshole who has to bear it, please. And—a-and! Th-then more assholes...will be saved...please—"

In the back of Steph's mind floated that scene at the beach. After the farce in the sea—Sora and Ino had faced off over who would groom her. And Izuna, who'd said she hated being petted by Ino, had nevertheless unhesitatingly—*headed right to him.*

—Grasping that this would be the last time...Izuna from the beginning had accepted this outcome. Through Werebeast's uncanny senses, they'd already understood one another. The only one who hadn't understood was Steph—but still.

"—Even so, you're sad, are you not?"

"I'm not...sad, please—I just don't...get it, please."

Grinding her teeth as she spat it out, Izuna, voice quavering, managed her question.

"...'Cos Soraaa...said no assholes would die, no assholes would suffer, please! ...So why, so why is it—I'm suffering, please? Is there some shit wrong with me, please...?!"

—Dripping, dropping. Izuna's voice made it clear even in the darkness that heavy tears were falling from her eyes. Yet Steph, conversely, felt the blood rush from her head. Izuna Hatsuse—she was too much a child. Too obedient, too innocent, too intelligent—too perfect a child. That this girl, at the tender age of eight, was forced to play games she didn't even want to play... To feel guilty having fun, to shoulder the weight of the continental domain, Steph realized something.

—For the Eastern Union to go about things this way—*was not a new development.*

—For them to cast off the few for the sake of the many—*was how things always were.*

"So this is the Eastern Union, making their children cry—this won't do at all."

—How Werebeast, said once to have been split into any number of tribes that were in constant conflict, had been united in just half a century and elevated to the status of a great nation—Steph seemed to glimpse it as she accused the Shrine Maiden—contemptuously, even. But the Shrine Maiden took her gaze head-on and answered.

"For the few to be sacrificed for the sake of the many—*is not even a necessary evil.* It's fate, lass. For all to have a jolly old time together, those are fine words—but a state won't run just by everyone bickering for what they want...dearie."

...Steph had no counterargument. In fact, that was just how it had been when she was dealing with the lords of Elkia. However you might try to keep anyone from losing out, perfect equality was unfeasible. As Steph clenched her fists at this truism, this time it was Jibril who rained down another blow. She looked as if she was asking sincerely, seemingly unable to comprehend Steph's argument.

"Dora, what is it that dissatisfies you? One life will be enough to save two races on the brink of destruction, fatten up Elkia as a nation, and even bring the federation with the Eastern Union closer to fruition—for what more could you ask?"

—Steph, still, had no counterargument. *Of all things*—Jibril continued.

"Did you think it was possible to take over the world—no, even take back Elkia's national borders—without sacrifice or discontent?"

"................!"

"Or is it simply—"

Jibril inquired with a still more provocative smile.

"—that you wish no suffering to come upon those close to you—that you wallow in the depths of narcissism and egotism? ♥"

Steph ground her teeth—she knew. The sacrifice of just one would win two races. It also meant that they would save two races that would have perished left on their own. If she felt that Ino's lone sacrifice was not worth it, then—

"——Then, so what, may I ask...?!"

But Steph opened her mouth decisively, and with the quivering Izuna in her field of vision, defiantly—she shouted, "Egotism, narcissism, you can call it what you like, but this much I can tell you! Uniting all the races by this method—is *never going to happeeen*!!!"

—She had no logical evidence. The Shrine Maiden and Jibril were right. Probably, indubitably. They were realistic. Yet, even so, for some reason, the conviction they were wrong held Steph fast. Why—it was, yes, probably, one might suppose—because they were plausible. Their words were plausible. Appropriate. Right on the mark.

—But to begin with... *The existing mark would never be enough—to unite all the races—*

■■■

As Sora and Shiro returned, wiping their hands, faces relieved, they were greeted by a departing Shrine Maiden, a heavy atmosphere. And—a piercing look from Steph.

"Uhh...what's the deal here?"

"So, essentially, you mean to *run*."

"—Uh?"

"I understand perfectly now. You'd get two races by sacrificing Mr. Ino—mere bluster... I've lost what faith I had in you! And, with this, you dare claim you will unite all the races!!"

In response to Steph's vitriol, Sora scratched his head and asked his sister confusedly:

"Uh, umm. Shiro, why's she yelling at me?"

"...'Cos...we took too long...?"

"It didn't take long. Come on, this is number one we're talking about! W-well, whatever, we got our business done, anyway."

—Clearing his throat once, *Ahem*, Sora muttered, "Let's get back on topic—

"So, it's that time again—*we're gonna go wake up that queen*."

......—What? To the speechless gathering, while yet ignorant of the discussion that had gone on in his absence, Sora calmly continued.

"If we can forget about Plum's magic and *actually wake up that queen on our own*, then Dhampir and Siren will both be saved, we'll get Ino back using that as a condition, and everything will be cool. I mean, we just 'exited' that game, you know. It would go against our principles to 'quit' it. So, now we have to stage our comeback—"

Disregarding the dazed crowd, Sora put his hand to his chin, ruminating.

"Question is, how can we actually wake the queen up—huh."

Ffp—sharply setting his gaze on Plum.

"Yeah, let me guess—*there's no one who knows the conditions...* right?"

"...Y-yeeess..."

"Wha—no one knows...what do you mean?"

Steph glanced at Izuna. For her part, Izuna (who'd been crying until very recently) now had her head raised as if intensely interested in Sora's words. She cautiously checked Plum's reaction—and then shook her head to indicate the Dhampir wasn't lying. But Sora nodded at an answer he'd seen coming.

"Siren can't use magic, and Dhampir can—if anyone knew, the lid would have been blown off long ago. Even Amila probably only knows that it's not a game to make her fall in love."

"...What gives you such confidence?"

"When Her Majesty went to sleep, she was not yet the queeeen... buuut, she was in a position to someday become the queeeen... If one such as that were to say she'd grant all of her rights...what would you dooo?"

Plum, who'd thought she'd *uncovered that*, spoke with a sigh. Sora and Shiro simply nodded.

"That's pretty chancy. If there was someone in a position like Amila's back then, she woulda *covered it up*—and what's the ultimate way to cover something up?"

"...*If no one...knows...the truth...no one will...know.*"

—Right, in other words... To beat the queen's game, you had to uncover conditions that no one knew except for the sleeping queen herself. It was—the victory condition game. Practically impossible. You could pretty much say it was hard as was conceivable. But——

"As long as it's not the real-life romance game—Blank doesn't lose!"
"...Mm...!"

Hearing the siblings' strong assertion—hard to judge whether powerful or pathetic, but self-assured in either event—Steph asked trepidatiously:

"...Uh, um... Sora, I thought you were abandoning Ino...... You're not?"

"Whaaa? What the hell are you talking about, *you friggin' Steph*?"

—To an extent, it didn't even bother her that her name had been employed as a direct insult. Sora's reaction represented a clear denial.

"There's no way I could do something that would make our living cultural heritage, Izuna, sad, and obviously I couldn't abandon Ino—that man among men. ...Steph, I know all this must be tiring for you, but can you wait until after you wake up for your half-lucid babbling?"

...Apparently, Sora had indeed raised his opinion of Ino into the stratosphere. It hadn't been an act. He went on.

"I mean—we said, *'We'll be back,'* right? Amila's not going to mess with Ino. 'Cos he's the only card she's got to get us to resume the game. If she touches Ino, then they'll really be doomed to be livestock."

Steph protested. "S-still, the Shrine Maiden said 'there's naught to be done' about Ino..."

"Well, yeah. We had the Shrine Maiden send Ino for verification. *Now the rest is our job.*"

At Sora's casual rebuttal, Steph's eyes widened. Indeed, as far as the Shrine Maiden was concerned—there was indeed *naught for it.* For momentarily—Sora and Shiro would grab everything.

"The Shrine Maiden's used the hell out of her bloodbreak, a power that threatens her very life, and even given us one of her most valuable officers. Now it's time for us to go at it like we wanna die— literally laying down our lives, you know."

Sora said it blithely, and Shiro nodded just as much so. But—their vaguely chilling resolve and next words took Steph's breath.

"That's what it means—*to fight together*, right?"

A little shadow slipped past the dazed Steph, approaching the siblings. Eyes red and swollen, Izuna, her gaze still quivering uneasily, looked up at Sora and Shiro.

"...You're gonna go save Grampy, please?"

Sora and Shiro didn't know why Izuna had been crying. Still— Sora placed his hand on Izuna's head, stroked it reassuringly, and smiled.

"Of course. We're gonna get your gramps—I *promise.*"

Her uncomposed eyes then turned to Shiro, where they were greeted with conviction.

"...Izzy...trust Brother..."

Izuna couldn't know. What only Shiro knew. What she *had* when Brother—when Sora—said the word *promise* signified an absolutely binding oath that made the Ten Covenants *worthless* in comparison. But—

"...Brother never...goes back, on his promises..."

At Shiro's assertion, Izuna once again looked up at Sora. The powerful hand stroking her head as she sniffed its scent...and then—she wiped her wet eyes.

"'Kay, I trust you assholes, please."

"All right, she trusts us assholes, please."

Steph watched the clowning Sora from a short distance away. Jibril stood next to her.

"My apologies, Dora. Our teasing was a bit immoderate."

"...What?"

"I was just so aching with curiosity as to how you would react, I couldn't help myself... But *you are in fact right, little Dora.*"

—So said the curiosity addict with a countenance that seemed to want to say, "Tee-hee! =P." But before Steph even had a chance to look sarcastic, Jibril got herself together, asserting:

."There can be no doubt that my masters are to reform this world." *But as for their methods*—Jibril continued, "No existing methods, indeed, could possibly serve the purpose."

".............."

So, now, as to how we're gonna uncover the conditions to wake up the queen—As Sora reinitiated his scheming, Steph only half-listened.

...Before, what the Shrine Maiden and Jibril had said—it had felt wrong to her. Steph, having searched for the reason—now seeing the two before her eyes—finally realized what it was. Sora...Shiro... these two never once used the *appropriate method.*

After all, conventional wisdom was something to be derided. After all, common sense was to be cast off. These two...said they'd conquer all the races bloodlessly, without a single death. With such a dreamlike—such an unrealistic—argument, there could be no conventional wisdom.

But, in his form that had made her believe that they could really do it, that day—the day of the coronation—Steph felt she'd seen it. Perhaps it was the same thing Jibril standing beside her saw—

—What she'd foreseen was this world's future, and it made her heart race, she realized.

"Oh, by the way, Steph. A minute ago, you said something I can't let slide."

"Huh?" Sora's words brought the dazedly ponderous Steph back to reality.

"About getting two races by sacrificing Ino—first of all, the part about sacrificing Ino is wrong. And also—"

—and here she got jammed right back into a daze.

"It's not two races—it's three!"

⋯⋯

⋯⋯——Come again?

INTERRUPT END

The exchange audible from the beach, felt at her back in the dusk as she walked, looking up at the moon... The Shrine Maiden muttered.

"...Did he know I was testing him—I wonder...?"

No...the Shrine Maiden gave her head a contemptuous shake at her own whisper. Whether he'd known or not, his actions would have been the same. Sora, from the start, had no mind at all to abandon Ino. His heartbeat, from start to finish, resounded pleasantly, without a single note of discord.

—Yes, the Shrine Maiden had been testing Sora and Shiro. What would she have done in their place, faced with the same decision? Probably—no, certainly—she would have chosen to cast Ino off. Because it would have been an unnecessary risk. Because, by sacrificing one, she would obtain much more. Because to ask for more than that would be idealism. And because casting aside such idealism—

—had been her limit.

"...Perhaps I can lay my hopes in them?"

Those two sneered at her limit and flew over it. Having sought confirmation of this—by testing whether they would save or abandon Ino—the Shrine Maiden closed her eyes. It was because—if

Sora and Shiro had abandoned him as she would have, for seeking more than her own limits in Sora and Shiro and giving them such a reckless test—

—she would have condemned herself till her last days. That was why she'd picked Ino, but—

"...Truly, I may be able to lay my hopes in them."

Having come this far, the Shrine Maiden finally understood. The noise at her back—Immanity, Werebeast, Flügel, and Dhampir.

—Those two had no concept of the barrier of race.

"...With those two—I may be able to leave it to them."

Thus, pressing her hand to her chest, the Shrine Maiden felt the throbbing of her heart—emotion long since forgotten. She looked up at the bloodred moon and whispered.

■■■

"Jibril."

"I am here."

Jibril shifted instantly behind Sora at his call.

"You...knew the story of why the queen is sleeping and even the condition to wake her up, right?"

It had been Jibril who'd told him, back when they'd met Plum.

"I did—except that I was mistaken..."

Misinterpreting his query as a rebuke, Jibril humbled herself before him. However...

"That's not my point. Where'd you get your info?"

"It was in my homeland—Avant Heim."

Then, half in hope, half in disgust, Sora continued.

"...We're talking about the Flügel here. You guys must have all kinds of books snatched up from all over the world, right?"

"Why, that goes without saying!"

Jibril nodded with irrepressible pride. Grinning a bit disgustedly at that face of hers, Sora thought, *Ah, whatever*, and moved on.

—To beat the queen's game. There couldn't be very many ways to root out an unknown, absent victory condition. But—there had to be a way. What they needed—for now—was information. And—

"Steph. You go work with Izuna and pore over the old king's library."

"—Huh?"

"Elkia's former continental territory was adjacent to the waters of Siren," explained Sora. "Considering that old king uncovered the Eastern Union's game, I can't imagine he didn't do any digging into his neighbor."

The man who had played the proud fool king—it was hard to suppose that he had a definite answer. If he'd pinned it down, then he should have woken up the queen himself—but—

"...Even if he doesn't have the answer, there's a high probability he left some thoughts on it."

Sora's eyes conveyed confidence in the king, Steph's grandfather.

"I'm counting on you, Steph."

"—Why, yes, Sir. You needn't worry."

"...Understood, please."

Together, Steph and Izuna each gave a big nod.

"...Uh, umm...S-soo, what are we supposed to dooo...?"

"Good point. Jibril. Take Shiro and me—and, Plum, we're taking you, too."

"Uh, a-all righhht... Huh, where are we goiiing...?"

"Didn't I tell you? —We're getting not two races, but three."

And Sora continued, beaming.

"Now, here's the question. To blow the lid off this game of unknown victory conditions, the most efficient approach is to dig up all the records we can about the queen's game as it's been played in the past and compare them against one another to deduce the principles—so, then, among all the places we could go, where would have the most records?"

...

—A moment's pause. And then. *Kshhrrrk*, two wills—perfectly contrary to each other—roared out.

"At last—at last! The new lord to reign over the Flügel shall finally grace his throne above us—oh, that this blessed day should visit so soon!"

"NOoooOOOOoo, no, pleaaase! Anywhere but that den of monsterrrrs!"

The sounds of Jibril, kneeling so fast in prayer as to kick up sand, and Plum, first wailing and trying to flee only to be caught by Jibril while struggling. Yet both were ignored by Sora as he took Shiro's hand. Nodding subtly, he spoke:

"Come, let us go—to Avant Heim."

TO BE CONTINUED

AFTERWORD

Wheww. I'm tired. ^__^ It's all done!

Actually, how this got started was I got asked to do the stuff I joked about in the preview in the last volume for real.

I didn't really have the story for this. ←

So I figured there was no sense in trampling over everyone's good-will and gave a shot at giving 'em what they wanted...lol.

Now a word to you all from my editor—

. Editor S for Sadist the Second: Mr. Kamiya, please desist from your thuggish disregard for professionalism. If you weren't doing both the text and illustrations, the original deadline would have already been a one-month extension. Also, I suggest you limit your Internet copypasta to about three lines at most.

—I'm sorry. I'll be serious. This is Yuu Kamiya. *No Game No Life* is back after five months—one month after it was originally supposed to be released. First of all, let me apologize deeply for the delay.

"Please feel regret. Deeper than the Mariana Trench."

Let me also mention that another reason the book was delayed was that my editor drastically misunderstood how it was going.

"I feel regret. Deeper than the lower mantle."

So, thus we have *No Game No Life, Volume 4.* Just as announced, it was my intention to make this volume fluffy and lighhht. After all, the threads going through Volumes 1 to 3 have all come together for now. So I planned this volume as, on one hand, a run-up to future developments, and, at the same time, a fluffyyy, lighhht kick-back party volume—

...That was the plan, anyway. How did it get this way?

"If you ask what I think personally, I would like to mention that the first draft of this fluffyyy, lighhht volume was *over four hundred pages* and request an explanation of this *X-Files*-esque mystery."

...Well, yes, there's a reason for that deeper than the Gutenberg discontinuity. Would you like to hear about it?

"Deeper than the lower mantle? I'd be much obliged."

To be frank. Do you remember that *a certain editor* had me make a manga of this with my wife? And then I ended up spending over a week every month working on it, so now, practically speaking—I've gone back to being a *manga-ka.*

"......Um, well...you see..."

And then I ended up also writing on a different series the previous Editor S for Sadist approached me about. That one, well, it's co-written, so it's not actually that much work. But, with all this going on, the machine I use for work broke down. And I ran to buy a new one, and I got hit by a car and suffered a bone fracture. Since I was running short on money and it got me some damages, that's fine, I guess.

"...It...is?"

The problem was afterward, when my editor drastically misunderstood how the book was going and caused me to try to split it up into three volumes. But it took a lot of work to split it up, and splitting it in two was the best I could do, you see? Thus it was four hundred pages. But, if I just split that straight in two, it would cause problems with the structure, and, most importantly, it would lose the momentum—etc. So, given this situation, I went through many iterations of working over the structure and revising the text. What do you think? Is it as deep as the Guten-whatever-it-is-ity?

"It's the Gutenberg discontinuity. What shall I say? That's—quite the story. ♥"

Yes, but I'd also like your comment on how a large proportion of this calamity was human-generated. ♥

"There certainly are some diabolical editors out there... It's a scary industry..."

Yes, some editors are so diabolical as to say lines like that with a straight face... (*Voice trembling*) It certainly is scary.

—Well, human-generated calamity aside, there were a lot of other things that I haven't even written about here. There was blood in my urine, and I got yelled at by my doctor, and I decided to eat some Korean barbecue for once and got food poisoning, for instance.

...I'm going to spell this out just in case, but this is nonfiction, okay?

"Mr. Kamiya, I suspect you should seriously visit a shrine for purification?"

I have.

"...What?"

The Meiji Shrine before I got cancer. Then the Fushimi Inari Shrine after. This year I went to Kawasaki Daishi, but look how that turned out. If I hadn't gone, I suppose by now I'd be crossing the river into the next life. Oh, but, at the end of last year, I was updating my bank book and I saw that it said "0" in real life, so I guess I wouldn't have had the fare to cross the Sanzu... What is it that happens if you didn't have the fare? Do you still get to be reincarnated?

"Um, I don't think there's supposed to be that kind of system for salvation..."

With that—let's call it a day. While this volume's contents were lighhht and eaaasy (heh), it's a run-up to the dash—while this series did have its first peak in the last volume! This is to be exceeded! As I work to push up the pace once more, with your kind—

"Oh, Mr. Kamiya, Mr. Kamiya."

Uh, oh, yes, what is it? Just when I was wrapping things up.

"Your editor from *Alive* has inquired, *Is the storyboard done yeeet?*"

......

"Then there are those extras, and the copy for the pamphlet for that project, and—wait. Mr. Kamiya? Are you there?"

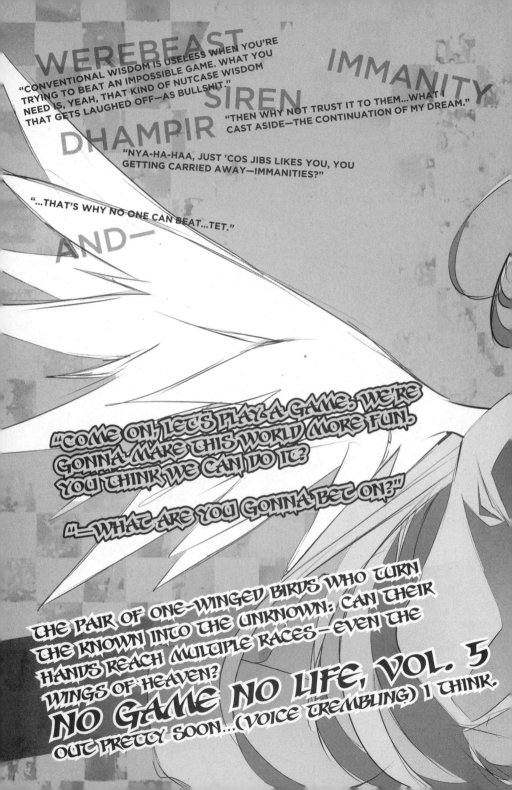

WEREBEAST

"CONVENTIONAL WISDOM IS USELESS WHEN YOU'RE
TRYING TO BEAT AN IMPOSSIBLE GAME. WHAT YOU
NEED IS, YEAH, THAT KIND OF NUTCASE WISDOM
THAT GETS LAUGHED OFF—AS BULLSHIT."

IMMANITY

SIREN

"THEN WHY NOT TRUST IT TO THEM...WHAT I
CAST ASIDE—THE CONTINUATION OF MY DREAM."

DHAMPIR

"NYA-HA-HAA, JUST 'COS JIBS LIKES YOU, YOU
GETTING CARRIED AWAY—IMMANITIES?"

"...THAT'S WHY NO ONE CAN BEAT...TET."

AND—

"COME ON, LET'S PLAY A GAME. WE'RE
GONNA MAKE THIS WORLD MORE FUN.
YOU THINK WE CAN DO IT?

"—WHAT ARE YOU GONNA BET ON?"

THE PAIR OF ONE-WINGED BIRDS WHO TURN
THE KNOWN INTO THE UNKNOWN: CAN THEIR
HANDS REACH MULTIPLE RACES—EVEN THE
WINGS OF HEAVEN?

NO GAME NO LIFE, VOL. 5

OUT PRETTY SOON...(VOICE TREMBLING) I THINK.

JUST ONE FOOLISH GAME—BUT THROUGH IT, CROSS THREE OR FOUR WILLS

A NEW GAME IN A BIZARRE
WORLD WITH ALIEN SPECIES!
PLAY, IF YOU DARE!

No
Game
No
LiFe

THE MANGA

Seven Seas